JOE R. LANSDALE

Winner of the Edgar Award
British Fantasy Award
Grinzane Cavour Prize
Bram Stoker Award for Lifetime Achievement

"A fresh discovery, three decades in the making!"
—*New York Times*

"Very Texan, very American, very funny—
and a stone brilliant writer."
—James Sallis, author of *Drive*

"Reading Joe R. Lansdale is like listening to a favorite
uncle who just happens to be a fabulous storyteller."
—Dean Koontz

"Lansdale is one of those very rare authors who can have
his readers howling with laughter during one sentence
while bringing tears to their eyes with the next."
—*bookreporter.com*

PM PRESS OUTSPOKEN AUTHORS SERIES

PM PRESS OUTSPOKEN AUTHORS SERIES

Miracles Ain't What They Used to Be

plus...

Miracles Ain't What They Used to Be

plus

The Parable of the Stick

and

lots of other stuff

Joe R. Lansdale

PM PRESS | 2016

"Doggone Justice," "The Drowned Man," "Darkness in the East," "The Day Before the Day After," and "Dark Inspiration" were originally published in the *Texas Observer*.

Miracles Ain't What They Used to Be
Joe R. Lansdale © 2016
This edition © 2016 PM Press
Series editor: Terry Bisson

ISBN: 978-1-62963-1-523
Library of Congress Control Number: 2016930967

Outsides: John Yates/Stealworks.com
Insides: Jonathan Rowland

PM Press
P.O. Box 23912
Oakland, CA 94623

10 9 8 7 6 5 4 3 2 1

Printed in the USA by the Employee Owners of Thomson-Shore in Dexter, Michigan
www.thomsonshore.com

CONTENTS

THE PARABLE OF THE STICK

LEONARD LOOKED UP FROM the newspaper he was reading, a little rag that was all that was left of our town paper, the bulk of it now being online, and glanced at me.

"So I'm reading in the paper here about how the high school, hell, grade school, all the grades, they got a no-fighting policy, no matter who starts it. Some guy jumps you on the playground, lunch break, or some such, and you whack him in the nose so he'll leave you alone, you both go to detention."

"Can't have kids fighting. You and me, we fought too much. Maybe it's not a good thing to learn, all that fighting. We met at a fight, remember?"

"Horseshit," Leonard said, and put the paper down. "Look here, Hap, I know a thing about you, and I know how it was for me at school, with integration and all, and I don't think it works like that, and shouldn't. This whole thing about fighting to protect yourself, and getting the same punishment as the one who picks on you, how's that teaching common sense?"

"How's it work, Leonard?"

"Think on it. There's this thing I know about you, let's call it the parable of the stick."

I knew exactly what he was talking about.

I said, "Okay, let's call it that."

"You moved here from a smaller school, and I know you had some problems. We've talked about it. I wasn't there, but I know the drill. Try being black in a formerly all-white school sometime."

"I could try being black," I said, "but I'd still be white."

"You came to school from some little town, to Marvel Creek. And there was this bully, a real asshole, bigger than you, and you were small then, right?"

"Not that I'm a behemoth now."

"No, you lack my manly physique, but you've grown into something solid. Then, though, you were a skinny little kid with hay fever and a plan to do something with your life. Which, of course, you failed to do. What were you going to be, by the way?"

"I don't know. A writer I thought."

"Ah, that's right. Hell, I knew that. It's been so long since you mentioned it, I forgot. Yeah, a writer. So you move here, a poor country kid with shabby clothes and his nose in a book, and this guy, this big kid, he picks on you. He does it everyday. Calls you book worm or some such, maybe pencil dick. So what do you do? You do the right thing. You go to the principal and tell him the kid's fucking with you, and the principal says, okay, and he pulls the mean kid in and talks to him. So what's the mean little shit do the very next day?"

"Double beats the shit out of me."

"There you have it, but you're not fighting back, right?"

"Oh, I fought back. I just wasn't any good at it then. Probably why I learned martial arts."

"Sure it is. I did the same thing. I wasn't so little and didn't lose too much, but I was a black kid in a formerly all white school, and then there was my extraordinary beauty they were jealous of."

"Don't forget the massive dick."

"Oh yeah, the black anaconda that knows no friends. So this happens a few days in a row, this mean kid ignoring the principal, him not giving a greased dog turd what the principal said. You go home, and your dad, he sees you got a black eye and busted lip, and what does he do?"

"He tells me if he's bigger than me, bring him down to size."

"Right. He says, 'Hap, go out there and get yourself a good stick, cause there's plenty of them lying around on the edge of the playground by the woods. You get that big stick, and you lay for him, and when he don't expect it none, you bring that sick down on him so hard it will cause you to come up off the ground. Don't put his eye out with it, and don't hit him in the head, unless you have to, but use that stick with all your force, and if something breaks on him, well, it breaks. You get a licking every day and you don't do something back, taking that licking and being licked is gonna turn into a life-time business.' He told you that, right?"

"Right."

"And you got you a stick next day at playground break, laid it up by the edge of the concrete wall on one side of the steps that led out of the school, and when the bell rang for the day to end, you got out there as quick as you could, ahead of the mean kid, and you picked up that stick."

"I did at that."

"And waited."

"Like a fucking hawk watching for a rat."

"Down the stairs he came, and you—"

"Swung that stick," I said. "Jesus. To this day I can still hear that fucking stick whistling in the wind, and I can still hear the way it met his leg just above the knee, right as he came down the last step. I remember even better that shit-eating, asshole-sucking grin he had on his face as he came down and saw me, before he realized about the stick. And better than that, I remember the way his face changed when he saw I had that stick. But it was too late for that motherfucker."

"What I'm saying."

"I caught him as he put his weight on his left leg. Smack of that stick on his hide was like a choir of angels had let out with one clean note, and down he went, right on his face."

"And when he started to get up?"

"I brought that stick down on his goddamn back with all I had in the tank, and oh my god, did that feel good. Then I couldn't stop, Leonard. I swear I couldn't."

"Tell it, brother. Tell it like it was. I never get tired of it."

"I started crying and swinging that stick, and I just couldn't fucking stop. Finally a teacher, a coach I think, he came out and got me and pulled me off that bastard, and that bastard was bawling like a baby and screaming, 'Don't hit me no more. Please don't hit me no more.'"

"I actually started to feel bad about it, sorry for him—"

"As you always do," Leonard said.

"—and they carried me to the principal's office, and they brought the asshole in with me, and they put us in chairs beside one another, where we both sat crying, me mostly with happiness, and him because I had just beaten the living hell out of him with a stick and he had a fucking limp. He hurt so bad he could hardly walk."

"What did the principal do?"

"You know what he did."

"Yeah, but now that you're worked up and starting to sweat, let's not spoil it by you not getting it all out, cause I can tell right now, for you, the whole thing is as raw as if it happened yesterday."

"It is. The principal said, 'Hap, did you hit him with a stick?' and I say to him, 'Hard as I could.' The principal looks at the mean kid, says, 'And what did you do?' 'I didn't do nothing,' he says. 'No,' the principal said, 'what did you do the day before, and the day before that, and what were you told?' And the kid said, 'I was told to leave Hap alone.'"

"And what did the principal say?" Leonard said. "Keep on telling it."

"You're nuts, Leonard. You know what he said."

"Like I said, I never tire of hearing this one."

"He said to the kid, 'But you went back and did it again anyway, didn't you? You went back and did it because you wanted to pick on someone who you thought wouldn't fight back, or couldn't, but today, he was waiting for you. You didn't start it today, but you started it every other day, and you got just what you deserve, you little bully. You picked on a nice kid that didn't want to fight and really just wanted to get along, and I know for a fact he asked you to quit, and he came to me, and I came to you, and still you did it. Why?' 'I don't know,' he said. 'There you are,' said the principal, 'the mantra of the ignorant and the doomed.'"

I took a deep breath.

"I remember him saying just that. The ignorant and the doomed. Then the principal said to me, 'Hap. He picks on you again, you have my permission to pick up a stick and just whack the good ole horse hockey out of him. I catch you laying in wait for him again, or doing it because you can, then that's different. That makes you just like him, a lowlife bully. He had this one coming, but he's only got it coming now if he starts it. But he picks on you, you give it to him back, and I won't do a thing. I won't say a word.'"

"There you have it," Leonard said. "That's the way we should have kept it. Self-defense is permissible."

"A stick was a little much," I said.

"Yeah, but these kids in school now, they're being taught to accept being victims. Why there's so many goddamn whiners, I think."

"That right?"

"You don't learn justice by taking it like the French. That's not how it works. Someone doesn't give you justice, you got to get your own."

"Or get out of the way of the problem."

"All right, there's that. But then the motherfucker just moves down the road a little and picks a new victim."

"I think you're trying to justify what we do sometimes."

"I don't need to justify it. Here's the thing, you get more shit from the meanies because the good folks don't stand up, don't know how, and don't learn how. And they're taught to just take it these days, and do it with a smile. Principal then, he knew what was up. You have any more trouble from the bully after that?"

"Not an inch worth," I said. "We became friends later, well, friendly enough. I think in his case it cured him across the board."

"So he didn't pick someone else to whip on?"

"No, but that doesn't mean it doesn't happen that way. I think he wasn't really a bad guy, just needed some adjustment, and I gave it to him. I think he had problems at home."

"Fuck him and his home," Leonard said. "Everyone now, they don't have an idea what's just, what's right, because they punish everyone the same. Ones that did it, and ones that didn't. I can see that if no one knows what went down, but now, even when they know who the culprit is, one who started it, it comes out the same for both. The good and the bad."

"Could have gone really bad. I could have killed that kid with that stick."

"That would have been too much, I guess," Leonard said.

"You guess?"

"All right, maybe too much, but there's still something to learn there, still something your dad taught you that matters and has guided you ever since. Don't treat the just and righteous as same as the bad and the willfully evil, or you breed a tribe of victims and a tribe of evil bastards. Learning to be a coward is the same as learning to be brave. It takes practice. And that, my good brother, is the parable of the stick."

APOLLO RED

Summer this happened, I must have been about seventeen, give or take a few months. I was down at the garage with my dad. He was washing tools in gasoline, cleaning them up, getting ready for me and him to drive to the café and get some lunch, though in that day and time we called the noon meal dinner, and the later meal supper. Yankees had lunch. We had dinner.

Dad was always greasy because he always worked. He cleaned up when he was home, but he was the kind of guy that could put on freshly cleaned and ironed khakis, and within an hour at the garage, look as if he had been living inside an oil drum. He worked hard and was good at it. He could fix any kind of car and make it hum. Odd thing was, we always drove junk. I guess it's like the barber who needs a haircut, the dentist who needs his teeth cleaned, the carpenter whose porch is sagging. Dad spent his time working on other people's cars, trying to put food on our table and a roof over our heads.

When he was eight his mother died, and his fondest mem-ory of her was that once for Christmas she had given him an orange and a peppermint stick. He talked about it like it had happened yesterday, like the gift was as important as a new car. For him it was.

His father was a mean-spirited jackass that made Dad work in the cotton fields when he was eight. At that time and place this was acceptable behavior. Once, on the way to the fields, Dad fell off the pinto pony he rode and busted his ear-drum. He rode the horse back home, hanging on its back, limp as a blanket.

His father took a horsewhip to him, then sent him back to work with blood running out of his ear. You'd think with an upbringing like that, Dad would have passed it down the line, but he didn't. I never got one whipping, spanking, whatever you want to call it. And I'll tell you, I'm not altogether opposed to a slap on the ass for doing something that is going to get you killed, but that's a far cry from a beating. I never got either from him, though my mother once took a flyswatter to me for some-thing I well deserved. It embarrassed me more than it hurt me.

For a poor kid I was what they called spoiled in those days, and what my mother called loved. Spoiled was going to work at fifteen instead of eight.

The summer this happened, I was working a night shift at Imperial Aluminum and going to school during the day, but this was the summer, so I was free until three thirty. I got off at midnight. If there were child labor laws against that, neither the boys I worked with nor the aluminum chair company we worked for was aware of it.

So there I was, waiting on Dad to clean up a bit, and this guy comes driving up in this shiny, gold Cadillac with a golden swan ornament on the hood, the kind that was made mostly of plastic. When you turned on the lights, the swan lit up. Coming down the road at night you saw the headlights, and dead center of the hood a golden swan floating across the night, seemingly pulling the car along with stiff-winged elegance. During the day it was just a gold-plastic bird with a wire and a bulb inside of it.

The Caddy drove up as we were about to leave, and this raw-boned, redheaded guy, with his short shirt sleeves rolled up to display his sizable biceps, got out. His hair was well-oiled and slicked back on the sides and he had a bit of a ducktail in the back. He looked as if he were wearing a copper helmet.

He got out and stuck a cigarette in his mouth, walked about halfway up to the wide-open garage doors, paused, lit his smoke carefully with a gold lighter—doing it for dramatic effect, like he was posing for a photo—and then snapped the lighter closed with a metallic clap, stuffed it in his tight pants pocket, and strutted into the garage, his black boots with red explosions on the toe flashing before him; the toes on those things were so long and pointed he could have kicked a cockroach to death in a corner.

The man kind of glowed. It was as if a white-trash Apollo had descended from heaven in his golden chariot, down from the sun to get his oil checked, have a chicken-fried steak with white gravy, and screw a mortal before ascending back to the heavens. In my mind I nicknamed him Apollo Red.

There was a lemon-colored Buick parked inside the garage, and it was the car my father had been working on that morning. Dad was drying his hands on a shop rag when this guy swaggered in, leaned a large hand on the Buick, and said, "This car fixed yet?"

Dad studied Apollo Red the way a snake studies a frog.

"Yep," Dad said.

"My girlfriend's got to have it."

"All right," Dad said. And he told the guy what the charge was.

"She'll have to owe you," said Apollo Red.

"Owes me for the last time I fixed it."

"Looks like you didn't fix it good enough."

"That was the transmission, this here was a leak in the carburetor. I rebuilt it so she don't have to buy a new one. I saved her about thirty dollars."

"Did, did you?"

Dad just looked at him.

The fellow strayed an eyeball my way. "That your boy?"

"Yeah," Dad said.

"Needs a haircut."

"Yeah, he does."

"I'd hold him down and trim it with a pocket knife."

I had heard this shit a million times, and sometimes it seemed a million times a day. Lot of the kids then had long hair. The girls liked it and so did I. I thought this hair remark was an odd statement coming from a man that wore his hair the way he did. Probably as long as mine, but tamed with hair oil and spray and a lot of mirror examination and a fine-toothed comb. I started to say something smart, but somehow I didn't want to get into Dad's bubble. And something about that guy made me cautious, like knowing to avoid a dark alley at night in a strange city.

"He might need it, but it won't be you cutting it, or two more just like you," Daddy said.

That caused Apollo Red to purse his lips and knit his brows. His gray eyes became slits. Apollo Red thought a moment, almost loud enough to hear his thoughts running about in his head like mice on gravel, and then he turned his attention back to Dad.

"Girlfriend needs the car. She sent me to get it. She can't pay you nothing right now, but she's good for it, and I'm going to take it."

"Naw, she ain't taking it, and neither are you," Dad said. "Shouldn't have worked on it, knowing she don't pay her bills."

"Is that right?"

"Know she works at the beauty parlor and has a long walk to work. Wanted to help her out, but I need at least half what she owes me for the last job. You got that, you can take it, though how you're going to drive two cars is a puzzle."

"I'll pull it out, park it in the lot, bring her to get it when she gets off work. She needs it tonight."

"Tell her to get the money," Dad said, and he was through talking. He walked by Red toward the garage doors. The doors were two wide metal sections you pulled closed and linked with a chain that ran through a hole in the doors, then you padlocked them together. Dad was about to pull the doors when Red said, "Wait a minute, old man."

Now at this time, Dad was pushing sixty, and that was back when sixty was old. He had gained a lot of weight and was tired-looking, but back in his younger days he had been a boxer and a carnival wrestler. He had a kind of strength, especially when he was younger, that was almost startling. It wasn't built-up gym stuff, it was working-man muscle, compacted and stretched and flexed by hard work from the time he was a child. He didn't look like much, but neither does a stick of dynamite.

That said, this guy was young and well formed, and he moved like a cat. Just looking at him, I knew he had done bad things and wanted to do more. I could feel a crackle in the air when he talked. It's that strange feeling you get when things aren't right, a sensation of something mean and nasty on the other side of some kind of dimensional barrier, waiting to get through a slit in time and space, enter into one of us humans and ignite our most evil traits, send us flailing with fists, snapping with teeth, slashing with knives, slinging clubs and tossing rocks.

Apollo Red, obviously annoyed, came outside and put his butt to the fender of his car, said, "You ain't going nowhere till you give me that car."

"Going to get something to eat," Dad said.

Apollo Red reached down and took hold of his belt with both hands and hitched it up, like maybe he was making room for a set of testicles the size of bowling balls, and said, "You ain't going nowhere, Greasy, less'n you give me that car."

"Soon as I lock these doors you can watch me and my boy and my greasy clothes drive away, cause I'm done talking to you."

This was like tossing gasoline on a fire for Apollo Red. "Tell you what, old man, I'll sort your shit out right now, that's what I'll do."

Dad looked at him. I had seen that gaze before, and let me tell you, you had to be a fucking idiot not to know there was something feral behind his near-black eyes, and that my dad was a man who had seen the devil and kicked his ass. But the devil had taken his beating twenty years earlier, not of recent from an overweight old man pushing sixty.

Apollo Red bounced himself off the car fender, cocked his hand back as he came forward, and I thought, Well, I'm stepping in. Dad's getting old, and I better help. But even though I was no slouch when it came to fighting, I was afraid. Apollo Red wasn't merely a smart-ass kid that wanted to tussle a bit. He was a bad man and you could sense it.

All of these thoughts came quickly, of course, and as I prepared to jump into the fray, Dad lunged forward. He was standing still one moment, and in the next he was covering ground like a bullet.

And then it came. It was an impossibly fast and short uppercut, but it was still a punch from hell. Before Apollo Red's punch could reach him, the uppercut rose, almost touching Red's chest as it tracked toward his chin. To this day I imagine flames coming off it, Dad was moving so fast. His shot hit while Apollo Red was still bringing his punch around. Dad's flat, fat fist caught Apollo Red solid under the chin, and it's the only time in my life I have actually seen someone lifted off the ground from a punch. That loudmouth was launched like a space rocket, and the only thing missing was a monkey on board and radio contact with NASA.

The blow made a sickening sound, and that uppercut lifted him onto the fender of his car. He rolled then, caught his shirt in the flying bird hood ornament and tore it half off, then rolled down onto the concrete drive. One leg starting kicking, like maybe he was trying to stomp a bug in a ditch, and then Apollo Red's head cocked back and he let out with a wheeze similar to steam hissing from a teapot. His eyes rolled up in his head like cherries in a slot machine. I almost expected him to spit coins.

And then he was still.

Corpse still.

I wouldn't have been surprised if vultures were already passing the word.

I went over, leaned down, and looked. Apollo Red's lips were blue. He may have been the sun god where he came from, but the god of lightning and thunder had just knocked the sunlight out of his ass.

I said, "Dad, I think you killed him."

Dad always carried a stub of a cigar in his shirt pocket, and as he walked over he pinched it from his pocket and poked it in his mouth. He scratched around in his pants pockets for a box of matches. When he found them, he took a match out slowly, struck it on the strike-strip on the side of the box, held the flame to that foul-smelling cigar. He shook the match and threw it down. He looked down at Red, turned his head from side to side like a curious dog, and said, "Nah. He'll come around."

I wasn't so sure.

"You hit him hard, Daddy."

"Man's punch is the last thing to go."

I guess Dad might actually have been a little concerned, because we didn't go to dinner. He stood near the guy's car for a bit, then went inside and picked up a comic book. He couldn't actually read, but he was learning a bit with western comics. He liked *Billy the Kid*. I sometimes helped him with the words.

"Go get us some hamburgers, Baby Man," he said.

I had anything but dinner on my mind, but in a kind of daze I drove to the café and got hamburgers, fries, couple of Cokes, and drove back.

This took about thirty minutes or so. Dad was still attempting to read his comic, moving his lips over the words he was learning. Apollo Red still hadn't moved. It had grown really hot.

Dad ate his hamburger and fries, then went back to work on a car at the rear of the garage, his head under the hood, whistling like one of the dwarfs from *Snow White*. Apollo Red, lying on the summer-hot concrete, still had not wiggled a muscle.

I tried to eat but couldn't. I stood and looked at Red. About an hour after he had taken a ride on the rocket from Hell, he twitched.

Like the Frankenstein monster testing his nerves and muscles, starting to recognize shapes and shadows, he writhed against the concrete. His jaw on one side had swollen to about the size of an eggplant and his chin had blackened like a two-day beard. The flesh around the eye on the side of the swelling had gone black as well. There was blood at the corners of his mouth.

Apollo Red stirred a little more. He rolled to one side with no more trouble than a beached whale. He lay there for a while pulling in ultraviolet rays. Birds flew over and dropped their shadows on him. Apollo Red finally got a knee under him, but his head hung low, as if heavy. The position he was in, it looked as if he were about to attempt an impromptu headstand. A tooth fell out of his mouth. He laid back down for a while.

I looked at Dad. He was still doping out the comic book.

Another fifteen or twenty minutes passed, and then Apollo Red moved again. He went through all the formations he had managed before, but this time, when it came to the knee position, he pushed up to his feet, wobbled a bit, and then forgetting he had come by car, started slowly zigzagging away, as if practicing evasive maneuvers against a slow-moving, heat-seeking missile.

He staggered across the street, over the dead grass next to the oil well bit shop, fell down, then got up with excruciating slowness, and continued to zigzag until he stumbled out of sight behind a high stack of tires at the rear of a filling station.

I finally ate my hamburger. Dad went back to work. I sat around for another hour. I had planned to eat dinner with Dad, go home, and go to work, but I decided the hell with it. I was too shook up. I walked across to the bit shop, borrowed their phone, called my boss, said I would be in late, if at all.

There was only one old man in the bit shop that day, and he grinned what teeth he had at me. "I seen him hit that sucker," he said, and pointed to a window in the side of the aluminum building to show me the exact spot where he had stood. "Damn. Bud's still got the punch, ain't he?"

"Yes, sir," I said. "Appears he does."

By the time I crossed back to the garage, a police car had pulled up alongside Apollo Red's golden chariot. There was a young policeman on the passenger side, and an older hand I recognized behind the wheel. He had once pulled me in for throwing water balloons. I nodded at him, like an experienced criminal acknowledging a foe.

The one on the passenger side, the younger one, got out as Dad came wandering out of the shop. Dad leaned against the hood of Red's car, which bore part of Red's shirt on the broken hood ornament like some sort of surrender flag. I came over and stood by Dad.

The young cop said, "Mr. Lansdale. There's been a complaint that you hit a man here."

"Hard as I could," Dad said.

"He has a broken jaw and is at the hospital and is a little confused."

"He was confused when he got here," Dad said.

The young cop nodded. "Well, sir, why'd you do it?"

"Threatened me."

"How?"

"Tried to hit me."

"Did he?"

"Too slow."

The young cop computed this, and said, "Sir, you have to come with us downtown. There's been a complaint. His girlfriend filed it."

"I don't think so," Dad said.

"You don't think what?" said the young cop.

"I don't think I'm coming."

The older cop behind the steering wheel leaned across the seat, and said through the open door, "Bud, you really got to come."

Dad turned his head in that curious dog way. "That you, Clyde?"

"Yes, sir."

"You know me," Dad said.

"Yes, sir," Clyde said.

"You know I'm not coming."

Clyde cleared his throat. "We're supposed to bring you in."

"Folks make plans."

The young cop, feeling the drift of things, stepped back and put his hand on his gun.

Dad reached out and gently pushed me away from him.

The older cop said, "Dean. Get back in the car."

Dean stood there with his hand on the butt of his revolver. He was sweating. The cop cap on his head seemed too big all of a sudden. I noted that the distance between him and Dad was not a lot different from the distance between Dad and Apollo Red when he had leaped forward and hit him.

"Dean," Clyde said. "Get back in the car."

After a long moment, Dean uncoiled and moved his hand from the gun.

Dad had not so much as changed his expression.

Dean got back in the car and closed the door.

They drove away and never came back.

Next day, when Dad went back to work, Red's car was gone, and about two weeks later the woman who owned the Buick came in and paid him all she owed, saying only, "How much?"

I was there that day, having dropped by to go to dinner with Dad again. The woman was a nice-looking blonde with a lot of hairspray on her hair; it formed a little blue cloud around her head when the sunlight hit it. I wanted to ask her if Apollo Red knew his own name and still remembered how to drive a car. I knew for sure he wasn't the one who had come for it. Apollo Red had descended, and would not be ascending for quite some time.

"It was the carburetor this time," Dad told her. "You might ought to think on getting some tires, too. These are may-pops."

"Yes, sir," said the lady.

Dad gave her the keys.

As she was slipping behind the wheel of her car, starting it up, Dad said, "Come on back, it gives you any trouble."

SHORT NIGHT

"ALL RIGHT, IT'S YOUR turn," Ed said, and lit a cigarette.

"I don't think so," I said.

"Everyone else has done her."

"I can see that."

The back passenger door of the car opened and Jack climbed out pulling up his pants, swinging his dong like the pendulum inside a grandfather clock. He took his time to tuck it into place behind his jeans and fasten his belt. He was pretty proud of his dick, and had the nickname Horse.

"I'm all done," Jack said.

"You was done before you got started," a female voice from inside the car said.

"I did all right," Jack said.

"Sure you did," she said.

Jack coughed and sidled off to the back of the car and leaned on the trunk and looked at the moon as if it were his job to study the arrangement of craters.

Ed put his arm around my shoulders and walked me to the car and the open door.

"You might as well knock some off," Ed said. He was kind of the co-coordinator of the event.

"It's all right, hon," Billie Sue said from inside the car. "I don't mind."

"I can see that," I said.

"Oh come on," she said. "I said I could fuck you all, and you're the last one left."

"Fuck Jack twice," I said.

"Ah come on," she said. "He barely managed it the first time."

"To hell with you, you old whore," Jack said.

"Flattery will get you nowhere," she said.

Jack walked away from the car to the edge of the woods and took his horse dick out again and took a piss.

I looked in the car.

Billie Sue was big and fat and her belly heaved. Her legs were spread and what I could see was less inviting than a leap into the bayou at night. You couldn't be sure what was down there. I looked away and felt ashamed of myself for being out there in the first place.

Billie Sue was married to a Baptist preacher, and she liked to take a break from gospel singing and collecting the Lottie Moon offerings to come out in the woods and fuck the senior class. Lottie Moon was a missionary who bothered the Chinese by trying to convert them. She was a kind of Baptist hero, but for me she was a long-dead busybody.

Billie Sue had been doing her own form of missionary work among each year's seniors for some four to five years. It was well known around town that she liked to bump with the boys, but her husband was said to give one damn fine sermon. The Baptists didn't want to lose him. And the knowledge of what his wife did made everyone in the congregation feel good about themselves. A little adultery and hypocrisy was easier to accept in oneself if the preacher's wife was considerably more wicked than they were. I thought that was nice. The Church of Christ had fired their preacher because he got caught dancing at a honky-tonk.

"Come on, kid, hop on," Billie Sue said. "I've got my second wind."

"No disrespect to you," I said. "Know you're trying to break a record, but I just came out here to see the stars."

"The stars?" Billie Sue said and laughed.

"Well, I didn't come for this," I said.

"Shit," Ed said. "You come for something, and it wasn't any stars. I think you ain't got the wood in your pencil to do it."

"Now that I've seen what I'm supposed to do, and who's gone before me, I'll admit there may be a severe lack of wood."

"You queer?" Billie Sue said, sat up and rested her back against the door on the far side.

"No."

"Free pussy and you ain't taking any?" Jack said. He had wandered back over. "That sounds queer to me."

"Jack's trying to get back on my good side," Billie Sue said.

Mike, a guy I knew a little, moved away from the other boys who were drinking beer near the back of the car, came over to me, said to Jack and Ed, "Leave him be. It wasn't any good anyway."

"Fuck you," Billie Sue said.

"I've had better when I didn't have any," Mike said.

"What's that supposed to mean?" Billie Sue said.

"It means it stunk."

"Well hell," she said, "by the time you was there, there had been eight others."

"That explains it then," Mike said. "Come on, Hap. Let's go."

"I didn't bring a car," I said.

"He came with me," Ed said. "I knew he was going to embarrass me like this, I wouldn't have brought him."

"It's all right," Billie Sue said. "I don't expect to be universally admired."

"You deserve respect," Ed said. "He can walk home, all I care."

"I got a car," Mike said.

I went with Mike and he drove us out of there in his '62 Impala.

We rode down off the hill, out of the night, into the glowing lights of the houses along the way, and then into the brighter lights of the Dairy Queen by the highway. Mike parked in the Dairy Queen lot and we went inside, ordered hamburgers and Cokes. Mike went to the bathroom while the burgers were cooking. I picked us a table at the rear of the place and sat down. There was no one else there but us and the cook and the fellow at the register. Ed came back, sat and said, "I really needed to wash up. I touched her a little. Not on purpose, but trying to guide it in, you know?"

"Okay," I said.

"I'm not trying to make you feel bad about not doing it," he said.

"I don't feel bad."

"She's okay with it," Mike said. "She likes it fine. It's a hobby."

"I know."

"She did ten guys last year, and this year she was going for twelve. She did eleven."

"Guess I messed up her record."

"She really had her heart set on twelve."

"Life is full of little disappointments," I said.

The burgers and drinks were called. We went up and got them and brought them back to the table.

"That stuff they said out there, about you being queer," Mike said, and turned his head a little when he spoke again. "You know, you're like that, it's okay with me. I've known a few. My uncle Bill was that way. One time I caught him sucking a schoolteacher's dick in our living room. He thought I was out, but I was in the bedroom reading. My uncle was a teacher too. He taught art. The guy's dick he was sucking, I don't remember what he taught. Speech or something."

"No. I'm not like that," I said.

"You know that colored fella you hang with?"

"Leonard?"

"He's queer."

"I know."

"It bother you?" Mike asked. "Not him being colored, but the queer part."

"Some at first. I guess I didn't know what to make of it. He seems like everyone else to me, except for the dick sucking part. He doesn't hide it any. I figure he'll get killed on account of it. Hell, I might get killed on account of it, I keep hanging around with him. I like him though. He's one tough sucker. He can be funny."

"I don't think of him as funny."

"He can be."

"I think it would take one tough customer to kill that nigger," Mike said.

"I don't think he likes being called a nigger. I'd stick with colored."

"That's something, ain't it. Don't call him nigger, but queer is all right."

"I think he does say he's queer. Says it plain and simple. I think he wouldn't want someone else to call him that, though. I know I wouldn't advise it."

"About the queer stuff, don't misunderstand me. I don't mind he is. Shit, right circumstances, I'd try it."

"What?"

"Sucking a dick."

"Oh."

"You?" he asked, and buried his face in his hamburger.

"Not on your life," I said. "I'm okay Leonard wants to do it. He's my friend. But I don't want no snapshots of it, diagrams and such. I like pussy just fine. Just didn't like that one tonight. I'm ashamed I went out there. I don't know what the hell I was thinking. I sure wouldn't want my girlfriend to know I went out there."

"You have a girlfriend?"

"Not right now. But if I had one, I wouldn't want her to know."

"Course not," Mike said, and nodded his head. "Understand, I was just posing a possible situation. A what if. I wasn't suggesting you and me might do such a thing. Suck each other's dick, I mean."

I got it then. I said, "But you fucked her."

He cleared his throat a little and took a sip of Coke.

"Yeah," he said. "Sure. It was fine. She was fat and a little sticky, but it was fine. I didn't mean what you think I meant. That wasn't what I was talking about. Not really. I was just talking."

"Sure," I said.

"Don't say anything to anybody," he said. "They might get the wrong idea."

"No problem."

"Hey, I'll drop you off."

"Thanks," I said.

We finished our burgers without talking and went out to his car.

He drove us away. He knew where I lived.

"How about the team this year?" he said. "I think we're going to stomp shit out of Mineola."

"It could happen," I said, as if I knew the first thing about football. I'd been to one game and that was so I could watch a girl I liked lead the cheers. She left with a football player and I left with some popcorn.

When Mike pulled up in my yard he cut the headlights so they didn't shine in the house windows and stir my parents. I opened my door, and that turned on the overhead light. I said, "Thanks for the ride. See you later."

"Hey, just to be clear," he said, "I was just kidding earlier, but it might have sounded like, you know—"

"No," I said. "It's good. I get it."

He looked at me there in the glow of the overhead light. He knew I got it all right.

I wanted to say something else to him, but I couldn't come up with anything. I closed the door and he drove away. It was, for a weekend, a short night.

I saw him at school after that. He always smiled and said hi, but he never sat with me at lunch, and he didn't spend any time with me when we crossed paths. After a while I didn't see him around anymore and I heard later from Leonard that he moved off to some place up north with his family.

MIRACLES AIN'T WHAT THEY USED TO BE

It was my original intent to write this as a well-measured, reasonable, and not at all angry or sarcastic piece on people who believe in religious miracles.

It didn't work out that way. And I didn't stay entirely on target.

Hitch up your drawers, here goes.

Miracles ain't what they used to be, but according to those who believe in them, they're as common as a politician's promise, maybe more so. There's Uncle Willie who stroked out on the operating table, but came back after he got a jolt of electricity with the paddles, and now he's right as rain, back smoking cigars, eating greasy pork, watching the Playboy Channel and telling you how he saw angels on the Other Side, all of them properly clothed, mind you. He only looks at nudes here in this here world. He saw those folks on the other side while he was deader than a no-interest bank loan. The angels came walking down a corridor of light, beckoning to him, but he heard a voice say, "It's not your time, Willie. I was just fucking with you, and I'm sending you back."

Or there's Aunt Ethel who came in from the rain and accidentally stuck her wet finger against a light socket and blew out all her house lights and all those in the neighborhood, catching Mrs. Sanders next door right in the middle of a vibrator episode that spoiled her close-touch with temporary nirvana. (Talk about fucking up a real religion—sexual gratification.)

Aunt Ethel was sent reeling across eternity in a white nightgown and bunny slippers (why not?) to see the bright, white light in the tunnel and the friendly face of a long-dead relative, smiling like a Walmart greeter.

And then, of course, Aunt Ethel was jerked back, coming around on the kitchen floor in a pool of urine and a pile of shit. She was dead, she'll tell you. But the Lord had other plans (which he obviously didn't share with the grinning greeter in the light tunnel) and brought her back because she is just *so special*, so special that you have to rehear her story so often that you begin to think there is no justice in death if it can't be final, and that whoever said life is short has never been trapped in a room with Aunt Ethel and the glorifying moment of her near-death experience. Only a poetry reading can seem as interminable.

According to these kinds of stories, the angels waiting in that corridor of light are frequently people the part-time-dead folk knew when alive. Often, they turn out to be relatives, or close friends who have gone on before, and have not aged.

We don't hear as often from those not traveling toward the light.

Maybe their glimpse of the *other place* was too unsavory to share. Who wants to hear about the warm and greasy slopes of Hell, where sinners end up making fiery license plates for Satan's magnificent, flame-colored fleet of DeSoto automobiles? Why Satan drives a DeSoto is a mystery, but there you have it. If there's a God I think he'd drive a Prius, environmental concerns and all, though those Teslas are way cool and can run like a spotted-ass ape, as my dad used to say. I have never figured out how come he was so familiar with spotted-ass apes.

Besides, if a Tesla is good enough for George R.R. Martin, why not God?

But I digress.

However this near-death experience is perceived, it is almost always declared a miracle because Uncle Willie, or Aunt Ethel, or someone like them, was dead as a brick on the operating table, or lying cool in their own waste, or tangled in a car wreck, and have come back alive! God brought them back because he had work for them to do here on earth, work which very nearly always seems to involve annoying evangelism or writing another book about how Heaven is real and the Bible is the word, even though instructionally it's more confusing and contradictory than internet articles on understanding string theory.

Growing up, going to church, I listened to the preachers and did as they suggested. "Read your Bible."

Holy shit! That cured me of Christianity.

According to the Bible, homosexuality is a sin, but a large number of other sins are mentioned as well. There are also privileges, such as the right of a male head of a household to sell his daughters into slavery (providing the price is right), and there are even sections that say you have the right to stone your son or brother if they are drunkards. According to the Bible you can also kill people who work on Sunday. (After they have given you your change, I guess.) There are lots of instructions about not eating shellfish and pork, and so on, but most Christians aren't even aware of this long and tedious list. They only know of the Ten Commandments, not the hundreds of others.

You're not even supposed to touch pork, or a dead pig, let alone eat it, because it is considered an unclean animal; to touch it is sinful. Football players pass the skin of a dead pig around every Sunday, but you don't see the haters of homosexuals rising up from their shellfish dinners and pork chops to scream about this abomination. You don't see them admonishing their wives for wearing garments with two different kinds of thread, though the Old Testament expressly speaks out against it. Hell, even the New Testament is tough on pigs. Jesus pulls the demons out of a man and puts them into a herd of swine and causes the swine to run into the river until they are "choked."

What did those poor swine ever do to Jesus?

To continue in this vein, the Old Testament is against hybrids of any kind. Do not mix different breeds of cattle, do not mix different types of plants. And I hope you aren't eating Big Boy tomatoes, cause those babies are cross-bred, and eating them will put you on a juicy, tasty road to Hell.

But the news here, Old and New Testament, is that the Good Book is tough on pigs and anything piggy, including all manner of pig products. That would include pigskin snacks, pork sausage, a lot of hot dogs, as well as the aforementioned football, and—well, the list is astronomical. How many different kinds of threads are mixed into our daily fabrics? If you are making the case that you are a stern believer in biblical commands, then do you get to pick and choose the ones you like and discard those that may deny you some seriously cool outfits and interfere with your Sunday TV schedule, where you see two teams of millionaires not only passing a pigskin but violating the holy law about working on Sunday? Football is their job.

So what it generally boils down to is "Kill the queer and pass the football."

Suspect one thing in the Bible as bullshit, and you find yourself checking your shoes repeatedly as you wander through the theological pasture. This includes miracles. First, did they really happen; and if so, then why are modern miracles a whole lot less miraculous?

The miracle that allowed Uncle Willie or Aunt Ethel to come back to us is nearly always assisted by doctors with years of medical training and hardworking nurses, as well as the best technology the hospital can afford. This is given short shrift. The formerly dead visitors don't come back from their well-lit vacation saying, "Thank you, doctors and nurses." Instead, they thank God or Jesus. (The Holy Ghost goes wanting. That guy gets no respect.)

The usual justification for thanking God is that God used the doctors to do his will. If a person gets well, thank God and Jesus, and if it turns out bad, it was a heavenly plan.

You can't beat a religion that is always right, not matter how contradictory.

Little Johnny has a Lego lodged up his nose and the doctors can't seem to get it out, but if they do, God has answered prayers. If little Johnny expires with the Lego still up his nose, then it was God's will that he be buried in a J.C. Penney suit and tie, and since only the top half of the coffin has to be opened, you can save on shoes.

Sometimes, like my fictional Aunt Ethel, these so-called dead come around, having visited Heaven's gate without luggage, and having brought nothing in the way of gifts back from the greeters, not even a coupon for twenty percent off angel wings and golden halos, the latter being about as useful as a gimme hat without a bill. The wings would be nice, however. It would take you less time to get to Walmart.

These added things are not actually part of the Bible, but I think Walmart may eventually be added, as many Christians I know buy their pork and shrimp and mixed-thread clothing there, or hammers and nails so they can work on Sunday.

As for returning from the dead, if you suggest that it may not be so much a miracle as medical training at work, these celestial adventurers who have been cast back into everyday life are as offended and angry as a child who's been told by some snot-nosed kid that the Tooth Fairy is a crock of shit, and it's your parents who drink the milk and eat the cookies you put out for Santa Claus.

God is the adult Santa Claus, and what's weird, he doesn't even leave a quarter under your pillow or put presents under a tree. It doesn't stop people from praying for money and cars and houses and longer dicks, but he never delivers. Though if by some coincidence you end up with money from a dead relative and find you can in fact afford a double-wide and a week's supply of Tall Boys, God gets the credit, even though everything else you asked for was denied. Fact is, life's lottery works pretty much the same for everybody. Sometimes you land on red, and sometimes you land on black. Sometimes it's snake eyes, and sometimes it's seven-come-eleven.

If God can give us rain, he can give us storms and earthquakes and forest fires, as well as Justin Bieber and the Kardashians. If he's all-powerful and responsible for everything, then he's to blame or praise for everything. It's only fair.

You can't just decide he's praiseworthy for the stuff you like. If there's an all-powerful deity he plays both sides of the street—and he's not averse to luring you out into the middle of it when a car is coming.

So let's say Homer Smith has just survived a tornado in the mobile home park where he lives.

"Well, here's how it was. I was sitting there in my double-wide, watching *Duck Dynasty*, and I heard this roaring like a train, and I looked out the winder there, and, holy moly guacamole, but here come a big ole twister, black as the hole to China, a twirling around and around, and it jumped right into the trailer park. I seen there was a dog and a car in that twister and all manner of junk, everything except my ex-wife, which I admit, forgive me Jesus, I slightly hoped for, and that damn tornado wiped out the entire park, wadded up my trailer like an aluminum can and carried me away. I woke up in a ditch (always a ditch) and I was alive. Everyone else in the trailer park was killed, including a mother and her twenty-five children, bound up in a ball so you couldn't tell where there was a head or where there was an ass, and there was a college student torn apart, as well as some educated fellow about to get his doctorate in the study of heart surgery. He got twisted up like a butter rope. But you know what God done? He said, 'To hell with them people. I love Homer,' (which is my name, though some folks call me Home) 'and I'm gonna save his bony ass and three teeth' (one of them, a front tooth, is a little dodgy and hanging by a thread) 'because Homer is far more precious to me than children and doctors and college students and such who may do great things.'

"I got to agree with him, cause here I am. And I say to that, 'God, thank you for your kindness and your wisdom, and for killing the shit out of them other unfortunates but not me. Also, a couple of beers were spared, and I want to thank your happy ass for that as well. I drank them beers and looked at the heavens and the corpses in the driveway, and wondered at your magnificence. Amen. P.S. I did get my car dinged, so you weren't entirely on the money. I won't be in church this Sunday.'"

Okay, Homer is a real moron, but frankly, this isn't that different from interviews I've seen on TV with the survivors of tornados. Even smart and reasonable people tend to believe that they have been spared because God sees them as special, unlike those who now have a microwave up their ass.

As an example of a miracle, an otherwise sensible man once told me how he knew that God was in his camp—because there was a terrible storm that killed a bunch of people, and a tree had fallen near his car, but it had missed, and therefore God was on his side. If it had fallen on the car, I suspect he would have decided that that was God's will.

A lot of these survival friends of God remind me of those who claim to have been kidnapped by extraterrestrials. Aliens come down, snag some guy while he's throwing the meat to a stump-broke cow, and fly him off among the stars quicker than you can say, "Rock them udders, bitch."

"Uwhap," says one of the aliens, "get the salad spoons. We got us another cracker and a cow."

These alien abduction experiences are not always described as positively as surviving a tornado (which can really happen), but there is still about them this air of survivors being *special*. Of being highly prized, selected for anal probes and sperm donations, *chosen* and perhaps used to create a superior race of beings, half alien and half peckerwood. Big-eyed grays with their caps turned backward who can drive a pickup as well as a UFO.

As I have said before, I digress.

So God kills everybody in the trailer park but one, and this survivor praises God for sparing him, even though he sure as hell drove death's bulldozer over the rest of those folks. This is what we must call human conceit. If I survived a twister, the first thing I'd think is that I was lucky and the others weren't, and that it could have gone either way. But not the true believer.

God is indeed the adult Santa Claus, and for some to even consider letting go of that last little fantasy is as impossible as shitting a pile of gold coins. Now there is a miracle even I would like to see, though I would insist on nose plugs and the coins being steam-cleaned afterwards.

I remember my own personal devastation on learning that Santa Claus did not in fact live at the North Pole, drive flying reindeer, wear a red suit, and deliver presents. It was painful. I was told then that Santa lived in our hearts and that if you believed in him, Christmas was in your heart every day of the year.

Fuck that. I wanted a magical guy in a red suit who could bring me presents. This is the same sort of bullshit you hear when you challenge miracles. Every day is a miracle. A baby being born is a miracle. A bird singing in a tree is a miracle. True believers struggle to keep God alive in their hearts because many, I suspect, actually question the whole thing but can't quite let themselves go there.

All I can say is, painful as it was, I got over Santa, same as the Tooth Fairy and the Easter Bunny. I do want to point out that I was always suspicious of the rabbit. That was a hop too far for me. And finally, so was God.

Many factors led me to being a nonbeliever, but there were two that were critical. One was that you had to reject science and common sense to justify the giant Pie In The Sky. The other was that God is willing to allow the horrors of the world to continue,—that as a deity he is as judgmental as a Tea Party Republican and has less kindness than people I've known.

Yeah, I know. Jesus was all about forgiving, but most hardcore Christians embrace the Old Testament because it is full of hate and revenge and you get to read about stuff like mass murder, incest, rape, and war—not to mention some nasty poems written by King David about fucking.

Truth is, the gun-toting, tough-talking, warmongering Christians I know do not consider Jesus their hero so much as John Wayne. They don't want to turn the other cheek, they want to kill something. If it can't be a human, there's always a deer.

These are frequently the same people who insist that black people are naturally inferior because, once upon a time, one of Noah's son's saw him naked, spotted his balls, and a curse was put on him. Ham's dark-skinned descendants were henceforth destined to be slaves and basically have a hard time of it, since God is an asshole and thinks accommodating this judgment of Noah's is a fair thing to do. Really, this is justifiable punishment? Why not add to this curse a limp and weak kidneys and the inability to match socks?

While we're on Noah, lets go back a bit, to the ark, one of the silliest ideas since the pet rock. But like the pet rock, it caught on. Unlike the pet rock, it has not receded into the past.

First, you have to accept that Noah could actually build a boat that would hold all the animals of the earth, two by two. (And if God so hated pork, why were pigs spared? But never mind that . . .)

Noah's ark is one big boat. The *Titanic*, or an aircraft carrier, couldn't hold all the animals of the world, even if it only chose one of each species and left the platypus a life preserver and best wishes. And as Twain once pointed out, who gets to swallow and bring along the microbes? Now that's a job no one wants. I can just imagine the looks on the faces of Noah's kin as they waited for him to pick the one who was going to have to down all those microbes, not only the "good" ones but the microbes bearing all the fatal diseases.

Many Christians brag about how literally they take the Bible, but when confronted with this ark business, they make excuses. Well, God can do anything. He got them all on there. They were all made very small, like animal crackers, and one of the kangaroos had to squeeze up tight in the glove compartment next to the map and the emergency candle.

The stench of an ark full of shitting and farting animals, not to mention humans, had to have been tough. Rabbits must have been hopping all over the place. Of course, the fast multiplying rabbits could have been beneficial. "Hey," says Noah to his wife. "Nail one of them little fuckers with a hammer and lets have lunch; otherwise, I'm afraid I might break down and eat some pork."

Believe it or not, we will come back to miracles.

Jesus and Christianity, if you set the Old Testament aside, is supposedly about charity and forgiveness. But many Christians appear to resent the idea of charity for anyone other than a personal friend or relative. They have the view that if you are in bad situation, you must have done something wrong to bring it on. If you're black, well, there's that whole Noah's balls thing.

Social programs that help anyone besides them or theirs, are generally perceived as undeserved. Goddamn Medicare, they say, as they take advantage of it. They have earned it, they say, not those others.

Goddamn socialist programs. As they cash their Social Security checks.

Goddamn entitlements, as veterans cash their checks.

Goddamn beggars, as they cash their unemployment checks.

And so forth. They curse them without realizing that they actually benefit from a lot of socialist ideas mixed in with their capitalism. Hey, I'm a capitalist, so how can my benefits be socialist?

Much of this view grows out of Christian concepts. Hey, I am on God's side, but the rest of those bastards are freeloaders.

Those Others.

It's always The Others who bring ruin on the Us. For the white populace it's the blacks or the Latinos, now and again the Asians, or the Jews, and of course, the homosexuals, which many Christians have determined were responsible for 9/11. If they hadn't been out there butt-fucking, and had been god-fearing instead, at home beating their wives and drinking beer, divorcing on a regular basis (which according to the Bible is also a sin) God wouldn't have let that happen. He'd have stuck to disease and old age, wars, murders, and accidents to kill people.

These are the same charitable Christians who want to snuff out anyone that isn't a Christian, which is in fact an Old Testament tradition. I always think of Joshua, commanded by God to wipe out the Amalekites, happily complying like a mean kid with a sun-heated magnifying glass sighting down on an anthill and its unsuspecting subjects.

God, the All-Benevolent Bully, has Joshua and his army kill the men, the women, the children (including babies), the elderly, and the animals. I mean, hell, what did the children and the donkeys ever do?

However, things got better with time.

You see, at some point, God, who was always a little bipolar and jealous and cranky, got on Zoloft or some such and was thinking, Hey, I'll have a son (without getting any nookie, of course). I'll give Mary this child, and she can birth him, and then when he's about thirty, I'm going to have him crucified—one of the more painful ways anyone can die—and then I'm going to raise him from the dead, for a few days, anyway, and announce that he's the Savior. Those who believe in him will be given a key to the gates of Heaven and everlasting life. Anyone who doesn't believe, then I'll burn those fuckers crisp as crackers. You see, I'll still be judgmental and test people, because I can't divest myself of all the cruel fun I've had, Zoloft or no Zoloft.

Still, the New Testament as a guide to life is an improvement over the Old Testament. Jesus seems like a pretty good fellow, at least from the King James version of the Bible.

Can you really imagine the King James version of Jesus toting an AR-15, or hunting to kill something for fun so he can put its head on the wall and brag about it? Jesus is love. But does he wear camo, and is he a hunting buddy? Those are the important questions.

Maybe he does both. Consider this:

Even those who embrace a gentler form of Christianity ignore the fact that there were originally more than four books about Jesus, and some were less flattering than the gospels. Some showed how Jesus was in fact a killer, using his powers not for good but purely for mischief and vengeance. These books, called the Apocrypha, were deleted from the Bible and the later books were gradually revised to show a more spiritual and kinder version of God's son.

The earlier Jesus, the Jesus represented in the Apocrypha, seems to be right out of the Old Testament, with a vengeance.

One book of the Apocrypha, the Gospel of Thomas, deals with Jesus' youth. It's interesting to read the segments where Jesus gets pissed off at other boys his age. I like the phrase he uses: "Thou shalt not finish thy course." Then God kills the boy who has offended him. In another section Jesus himself kills a boy for throwing a rock at him, saying once again, "Thou shalt not finish thy course."

In another scene, Jesus is playing on a roof with some boys when one of them, pushed by another boy, falls to his death. The boys scatter, leaving Jesus to take the blame. And why not? The little bastard is already a known killer and a cantankerous asshole.

Jesus, to prove his innocence, has the boy brought back to life (nothing medical here; this was an instantaneous miracle) so he can explain what happened.

The boy, now breathing and well alive, says, and I paraphrase here, "Naw, J.C. didn't do it this time. We was fucking around up there, and Billy Bob pushed me and I slipped and smacked my noggin on a rock. That's what killed me."

This book was conveniently removed from the Bible, along with a number of troubling books that didn't fit the evolution of biblical ideas. (That's another human trait, changing things, attempting to improve them to fit one's own ideas.)

I will admit, out of fairness, that there's also something cool in those older books. In one incident, Jesus makes sparrows of mud and causes them to fly. That part is cool; the killing parts, not so much.

These books are still available and translated into English. Check them out. The Bible was changed constantly, and eventually we had the King James version, but it is merely one of several. Many scholars have been upset with how dramatically sections of the Bible have been altered over time. Even the monks of old were bothered by it, and wrote in the margins of biblical manuscripts brief instructions that amounted to, "Stop changing things!"

Good storytellers, however, will not be denied, so there were slight changes from one monk to the next, and in fact, some outright new inventions, one of which was the Old Testament Noah story. Or so the evidence suggests. "I been reading some Gilgamesh, and he's got a flood in his story, and some animal stuff, so why don't we add that?" says one monk to another. "Go for it," says the other monk. "It's a good story. Who gives a damn if it's true?"

As for the New Testament, the oldest version of it in existence, the Sinai Bible, does not contain Jesus' resurrection. This is the Gospel of Mark. Even the Catholic Church believes it is the earliest representative of the New Testament, and is the basis for other books, said to have been written later by Matthew and Luke. It appears obvious that Mark was not the only source for these later reconstructions. All manner of influences were soaked into those pages over time. They are story by committee, and if you've ever worked for

Hollywood as a scriptwriter, you know how this kind of stuff can turn out.

The obvious lesson here is that the resurrection was added in at a later date. As far as the Bible being written by Mark, or the later versions by Matthew and Luke, it could just have easily be labeled "written by Heathcliff and Amos" for all the true historical value there is. In fact, there is no mention of the virgin birth by Mary in this version, which immediately kills the whole kafuffle about Jesus being from the Old Testament line of David. He seems to be mostly from the line of Imagination.

Another sideline on that bloodline of David business: Outside of the Bible, there has never been found one bit of evidence that there was a David, or a Solomon for that matter. Historically they are as elusive as Hercules or a Blue Power Ranger with real powers. It's like the Hebrew slaves in Egypt, Moses, all of that story. Outside of the Bible, the evidence vanishes.

Not to put too fine a point on it . . . Oh, hell, let's do put a fine point on it. Jesus himself is suspect. He is mentioned only once in Josephus, the authoritative first-century chronicler of Jewish history. And then it's only as one of a slew of nuts running around claiming to be a prophet or messiah.

Jesus seems to have been given the mantle of divinity by those who followed him or claimed to have followed his disciples. Later versions of the New Testament added the resurrection and the virgin birth stuff. My view is that Jesus was born in the normal way, did good work, mostly charitable things, died, and didn't come back.

Another thing overlooked is that we know how old the Bible is, at least down to a few decades. For the Old Testament we're talking roughly four thousand years, and two thousand for the New Testament. This is why so many Christians argue that the world is not as old as scientists claim.

To accept that the world is in fact billions of years old, and that humans in one form or another have existed for something like seven million years, and in modern form something like two hundred thousand, makes their belief system hard to swallow, so they therefore declare that the geological and archeological timeline isn't true and that the world is no older than your great-grandmother's socks.

This brings about another question. All those folks before the Bible, what happened to their souls?

Are they outright forgiven?

If so, why so hard on the later folks?

If they're not forgiven, what happens to them? Are they just diddled in Hell? Do they get folding chairs and a sack lunch in limbo?

If good folks go to Heaven, do they stay the age they were when they died? Does Uncle Jim get better looking? Will Aunt Jane lose weight, or gain some? Will we all be in good shape? Is there sex in Heaven? If not, why go? Will our dogs be there? If not, why go?

I suspect all cats go straight to Hell.

Do you have to hang out with your brother who died as a baby? Is he given a heavenly pass or is he in limbo, having done nothing other than be born and then die? What sin could a baby have committed? Are AIDS babies given a pass? They never knew they were supposed to believe in this religion business. Why would they be punished? Why would God allow them to have had AIDS? Who is he punishing and why? If he's punishing the mother for having a child out of wedlock, for example, why does the baby carry the weight of the punishment? And that baby brother, what exactly are you going to talk about? Does he still wear diapers, perhaps now made of clouds? Who has to change him and powder his ass?

How does that work?

"God moves in mysterious ways," is the desperate answer.

Well, don't he, though!

All of this is by way of saying there's a lot of questionable business if you're going to embrace religion, and this should make the religions themselves suspect, which in turn gives the whole idea of modern miracles a noticeable stench.

Told you I'd get back to it.

It's all tied together. Blind belief in blind ideas, and true miracles go wanting. Faith is the answer normally given when Christians find themselves painted into a corner.

You have to accept it on faith, they say.

Faith?

The problem with faith is, which faith? Islam has faith and so do the Hindus. Even among Christians, each sect believes it knows the best way, and all the others are theological morons.

The Church of Christ believes it's right. The Baptists think they have the inside track. The Methodists (also known as Baptists who can read) think the have the inside track. And then there are the Pentecostals, the Jehovah's Witnesses, the Church of Latter Day Saints, Catholics, Episcopalians,

Calvinists, and so on. They all think they hold the proper cards. So which faith are we referring to?

Let's take a simple miracle test. You won't need a pencil.

Start with God, who can do anything.

Check? Powerful dude.

So, instead of just causing a miracle flat out, why does he use doctors to accomplish his miracles, and why do so many of these miracles require recovery time? Why do so many of them leave people maimed and scarred and missing pieces?

In the Bible miracles are instantaneous and absolute. Lazarus wasn't given a body massage by Jesus, electric paddles, and an IV full of go-juice and some cautious instructions. He just got up from his deathbed and walked out into the light. He had been dead for four days, which is right there in the Stink Zone. But he came out alive, full and whole, not a walking dead man but a living human being. At least according to the Bible.

But I digress. Back to the test.

How many amputees do you know who have grown back limbs?

What I thought.

Why does this particular miracle never occur? Maybe because this one can't be rationalized. Someone dies on the operating table and then lives, they can claim it's God's will. But for God to do an all-powerful and perfect miracle, like having a leg grow back . . . Whoops.

How many people who have lost an eye have grown that eye back?

Kind of a short list, huh?

But here's the real test. Let's have one of God's representatives come to a veterans' home and see all those maimed and wounded men, and with a wave of their hand call on God for a miracle. Let's see their burned and mauled faces, their missing hands and arms and legs, reappear in good form and fine working order. Have them all get up refreshed, repaired, and ready to go home.

That would be a true miracle, and easy for God to perform. Remember, he is all-powerful. God doesn't need no stinking doctors.

Better yet, God, end war. You have the power to do it, right? No?

Yeah, I know. Every day is a miracle. Birds sing in trees (when the hunter who loves Jesus isn't shooting them) and babies are born, and the season's change—

Stop it.

Let's do a real miracle, not some bullshit substitute, like Santa lives in your heart. Get real.

Signs in yards often say prayer is our only hope, so I assume those people are praying. Are they praying only for the little things, like, Please let me pass this chemistry test. "Oh, God, if you will make sure Janey isn't pregnant, I will be in church every Sunday from now on until I die, and I will never, ever have sex again without a rubber."

A new car in your driveway, or getting a raise at work, is not a miracle. Stopping global conflict would rate higher. That we could call a miracle.

Yet, God seems more interested in attending to petty needs while the larger issues of genocide, war, disease, rape, and murder go wanting. At sight of those atrocities, God seems to decamp in the night and slink off to keep a tree from falling on your used Buick.

But let's take this a step further.

So God brings you back from the dead. You're one of those who have seen the white light. Died on the operating table, and God brought you back.

Glad you're here with us, but you should thank the doctors and nurses.

Let's pick somebody who has been dead for several days and is starting to stink. The stinky dead, like Lazarus surely was, or was beginning to be. Let's pick some poor bastard who is found dead from some disaster. People crushed by falling buildings during an earthquake that you allowed, God. People drowned in a hurricane that you allowed, God.

Bring those dead folks back.

Have one of your representatives do it, if you feel it's too vulgar to do yourself.

Make the dead walk. You don't need doctors and medical care, God. You deliver miracles.

Call them out of their deadness and set dinner for them and start the coffee.

What? Too much for the all-powerful God? He only does that shit in the Bible, doesn't he? Or so it's claimed. Yet you're not one bit suspicious?

I know, there are birds singing in the trees, and babies are born, and these are God's miracles . . .

Go screw yourself.

I want these God-given miracles I hear so much about, not some weak-ass substitute. I want some of that witchy supernatural stuff.

Pull out of the bag that godly magic and put it in the light.

None of that "I saw Jesus' face in a tortilla" stuff, or in an assortment of flies on a screen door. Not so long ago it was claimed there was an image of Jesus in a grilled cheese sandwich.

Come on, God. Is that all you got?

Wait just a damn minute, here's something. This would solve all the problems of the world and religion in one fell swoop.

If God is all-powerful, why doesn't he make this a perfect world? I'm not talking a good meal, a perfect cup of coffee, and a fantastic bowel movement.

I mean more than that.

Make it perfect. Be kind to your creations. Oh yeah. You got better with that Jesus thing, but you know, you got a past, man, and I have a long memory.

But the *perfect thing*, that hasn't occurred to God? He's too busy giving us tests, checking his books to see who's been naughty, who's been nice, who killed whom, and who has gone over to the dark side by being for gay marriage.

God, if you're all-powerful and all-loving, and not just a thing in our heads, do it. You could prove your existence in an instant. You would have a revival to end all revivals and lots of people would be falling in line with your existence. Dancing in the streets would occur. Unless you're against dancing. Opinions on that are mixed.

Hell, you don't have to come down here yourself. Send Jesus, or the under-used Holy Ghost. (What the hell is he up to? Is he mostly the janitor in Heaven?)

To give it all weight, I suggest you or your son come down. "Here I am," says Jesus. "Everybody be happy. Everybody be perfect. Pull up your sagging pants and turn off that rap music. There you go. Now I'm back to the house. The climate change problem has really warmed this place up."

We're talking God-given perfection, which this all-powerful being is supposed to be able to do, other than give us all a lifetime of moral exams, putting obstacles in our paths, having many born without obstacles, some handsome, some born maimed or mentally deficient, some with good parents, some with terrible ones. In other words, God doesn't give us a fair playing field, but expects the same thing from everyone, no matter how hard and disadvantaged some of his creations might be.

God, being jealous and irritable, condemns the best nonbelievers to Hell alongside murderers, rapist, mimes, and Barry Manilow fans. To go to Heaven, you have to believe in God, not merely be a good person. You have to be willing to beg and plead for his acceptance, while a horrid child-murderer in prison can talk to a preacher, admit his sins, and be given life eternal.

Of course, we nonbelievers neither believe in celestial punishment or reward. It seems obvious that the all-knowing, all-loving God is little more than a celestial bully.

Look, I know there are plenty of Christians who practice the better aspects of Christianity. They know how, like a crow, to pick the corn kernels from the piles of cow shit. How to choose the better elements of their religion from the sludge pile of narrowness, hate-mongering, and shit-smoldering mounds of stupidity contained within.

I can go along with these folks, silly as I think their religion may be, if for no other reason than that they have a positive design. I respect their right to believe in something I don't, but I don't respect the religion. I don't respect any religion. I can respect the person, however, if they try to live by a good ethical code and actually practice kindness and forgiveness.

Not being a Christian, I don't do those things for a bunk in Heaven, but I do them because I think they are right and positive. I may fail, but I sincerely try. Not because I live in fear of offending an invisible, nonexistent being, but because that's how the best of humans should act. Not so you can hang out in Heaven with the Christian God, or have the Islamic male reward of seventy-two virgins (which frankly I don't remember actually being in the Quran, but maybe it is). But all belief in God or gods comes from the same source: self-delusion. And I will add this—virgins are not as much fun as you may think.

Sure, someone has to put that quarter under the pillow when you lose a tooth, or buy presents come Christmastime, or leave brightly colored eggs in the yard amidst chigger-infested grass. Someone has to teach you how to be a good person. But it isn't always someone of the religious ilk.

Desire for a life beyond this one is strong in our mortal flesh, but in the end, all of us are a blink in the "eyes" of the Universe, and all of us will be forgotten. It would be nice if the best of us received a reward, maybe a nice collection of soaps and shampoos, and the worst of us were punished. But the Universe has little interest in what happens to us.

What it boils down to is this:

There is no God.

I can live with that easily.

My rant is done.

"THAT'S HOW YOU CLEAN A SQUIRREL"

JOE R. LANSDALE INTERVIEWED BY TERRY BISSON

Where does East Texas end? (And don't say the Louisiana line.)

It doesn't stretch as far as Dallas, heading west, since that is what used to be called The Plains, though today The Concrete is more accurate. Simply put, if you go west and the trees disappear and the dirt gets black, you are not in East Texas anymore. Going north, it dies out before the Red River by some distance. Go southeast to Houston and you have gone too far. Houston is in the Coastal region, which though similar is still different.

East Texas has lots of shade, running water, and a meth problem.

Everyone (Hollywood included) agrees you have a gift for dialogue, but I think it goes deeper than that. There's a vein of indirection and understatement in all your prose that I identify as a southern thing. Just saying.

I think that's true, but East Texans can be very direct. It's said that we drawl, but if we do, we drawl fast. We speak faster than most southerners, and our culture is more southern than southwestern; and though those two overlap, we are more farmer types than rancher types.

I think one reason I do pretty well with dialogue is that we are storytellers here, or at least have been in the past, and that's a southern tradition. If the story has to do with somebody dead and their body tossed down into an old water well, or something dark in the woods, then all the better.

I always loved to listen to the older folks when I was growing up, how they talked. It impacted my writing by quite a bit. My parents were older when I was born, and they had gone through the Great Depression and therefore had a different viewpoint than the parents of many of the other kids I grew up with. My personal culture overlapped that of earlier periods, the Great Depression, and that of the fifties and sixties; in our family I was probably the only counterculture kid, so I have that to draw on as well.

My father had a lot of great sayings from having been born in 1909 and having heard as he grew up sayings from the 1800s. His relatives, many of them, had fought in the Civil War. My grandmother on my mother's side was close to a hundred years old when she died. Came to Texas in a covered wagon. Saw Buffalo Bill's Wild West show when she was a child and was forever enraptured by it. My father had boxed and wrestled a little for money, riding the rails to fairs to fight. He couldn't read or write, though at the end of his life he got so he could read a little—newspapers, comics, simple paperbacks. But he could never actually be called literate.

My mother was a great reader when I was growing up and encouraged me to read. So did my dad. He knew how hard it had been for him not being able to read or write.

I often hear that story, of how southerners are all storytellers. Sometimes I think it's just one of their stories. But let's move on. Horror and humor seem closely linked in your work. Does one drive the other or are they just fellow travelers?

I think they are fellow travelers, though it can work the other way as well. A lot of the old frontier stories my dad told were both horrible and funny. People of his era could slap their knees and laugh over some pretty horrible stuff, but they were also kind and helpful people. I think they had to laugh at the horrors as a way of survival. It was rough-and-tumble humor, the sort of thing people today would be aghast at. Rightfully so, I guess, but when Dad told those stories they tickled the shit out of me.

Mark Twain said there's no humor in Heaven. Meaning, nearly everything we think is funny is based on the misfortune of others, as well as ourselves. Bad things can be funny, mostly in retrospect. As a character in my novel *The Thicket* said, "Everything in life is humorous, except your own death. But others will laugh."

You often mention Edgar Rice Burroughs as a "sentimental favorite" and an inspiration. Yet your writing hews much closer to noir and modernist realism. Who were your first actual models, that you imitated, knowingly or not?

Burroughs inflamed my desire to write. He was the writer I originally imitated, and I think his headlong pace has stayed with me. I was already writing before I read Burroughs, mostly inspired by comics, *The Jungle Book*, *The Iliad*, and *The Odyssey*, Edith Hamilton's book of mythology. We also had the Bible and Shakespeare, and my mother gathered up books here and there, so I was always reading. But Burroughs set me on fire.

Later on my influences were legion. Lots of science fiction inspired me, writers like Philip José Farmer, Cyril Kornbluth, Fred Brown, Henry Kuttner, and a little later Ray Bradbury. And then Hemingway and Fitzgerald and Steinbeck, plus a little bit of Faulkner. Flannery O'Connor was major. I really didn't care for the Beats so much, but I learned a lot from reading Jack Kerouac, especially *On the Road*, which I liked. William S. Burroughs (the other Burroughs) put me to sleep, and I had to work to hard to get anything out of his cut-up style, which seemed more gimmick than story. I think at heart I'm a storyteller, and I want my style to accomplish that, which doesn't mean I can't be experimental.

I was also heavily influenced by Chandler, Hammett, James M. Cain, tons of noir writers, and many who wrote for Gold Medal. Those Gold Medal novels were mostly short and swift, and you could easily read one in a few hours. On weekends I used to devour two or three after morning martial arts practice, which is something I've also done for a long time. Over fifty years.

If you were to pick one book or story that "launched" you, what would it be?

For me it was a one-two-three punch. In 1986 *The Magic Wagon* come out, and it was reviewed well and treated like a literary novel, which gave me those creds (for whatever they are worth). *Dead in the West*, a pure pulp novel, came out the same year and started a sort of underground or small-press run that continues along with my mainstream publishing run to this day. "Tight Little Stitches in a Dead Man's Back," though it was not my first short story, got me a lot of attention and a nomination for the World Fantasy Award, which it didn't win (though I see places where it says it did). I've been nominated for World Fantasy many times, but no wins, so I'm correcting that confusion here. That story gave me my short story credentials. I also sold a nonfiction book that year that didn't come out until years later. Anyway, I made some money that year, and I started a three-pronged career in prose that's continued until this day.

I was introduced to your work by The Drive-In. *Is there a drive-in in Nacogdoches? Did you ever wonder what happened to all those little pot-metal speakers?*

I have wondered about those speakers. Once they switched to the radio, it was never the same again. I loved drive-ins. I don't know how much I would love them now, the heat and mosquitoes might not be too appealing these days. We had a drive-in in Nacogdoches, and we went often, but most of my Texas drive-in viewings were in Tyler, Kilgore, and Longview.

Back then they had movies made especially for drive-ins, things you couldn't see anywhere else. Most were terrible, but many were perfect for the young mind in search of horror, female nudity, and gratuitous violence. They also gave us a private place for sex, and talking about the sex we weren't getting. The popcorn wasn't too good. Always tasted like wet cardboard.

Your "Miracles" piece is pretty hard on religion. I get that. Were you raised as a Methodist or a Baptist?

Baptist. I actually am not against religion itself, but when people use it to justify bad behavior, or when they show how hypocritical they are, I always wonder if they've read the Bible they love to quote and shake. To justify some of the things many Christians justify, by quoting it selectively, irritates me. I don't believe there is a god, outside of the blind, uncaring power of nature. I don't mind Christians who try and live by the better attributes of their religion, but it seems to me, especially in the South, that most of what they get from the Bible is just the bad stuff. Reason for that is, it's mostly bad stuff.

The New Testament has its more positive side, but basically if you believe *Do unto others as you would have them do unto you* and know the Beatitudes, you can forget both books and, for that matter, Jesus. Thinking some guy who died over two thousand years ago is coming back is not much different from older religions that we now think of as mythology. So, yes, I can be rough on it.

Who taught you to drive? To write?

My dad and mom both taught me to drive, mostly my mom. My uncles a little. I taught myself to write from reading. I never had a course in creative writing, though I've taught a few, and am writer-in-residence at SFA [Stephen F. Austin State University]. I don't think you can make someone a writer. You can assist them and open a few doors, but it's always up to the person. Some people just have It. Others may know the alphabet, excellent grammar, and spell perfectly, but they seem to be trying to light a match underwater. It's just not there. I don't know why that is, but it's usually that way. Now and again someone, like Robert Johnson, who couldn't play the guitar worth a damn, will go off and come back a virtuoso, but that's rare.

Were you a fan of Bruce Campbell before Bubba-Ho-Tep? *Do you ever have any say in the casting of films from your work?*

I was a fan. My son Keith was a fanatic fan. He loves him some Bruce. He begged me to get Bruce for *Bubba*. I told him that wasn't my call, that was Don's call [producer, director Don Coscarelli]. Don called me one day and asked, "What do you think about Bruce Campbell?" and I laughed out loud.

Keith and I went on the set and met Bruce and Ossie Davis. We already knew Don and the other actors and people working on the film. Nice experience.

Bruce and I have been friends ever since. He's like the Elvis of B movies, but the thing is, the man can act. I've never thought he got his due. *Bubba*, in my view, is his finest performance, and Don's best film so far.

I was fortunate enough to meet Neal Barrett Jr. and even hung out with him (in Greenwich Village, of all places) but we never worked together. How'd you get so lucky?

Neal Barrett Jr. was a brilliant and neglected master. He wrote some survival stuff, but the best of his work, like *The Hereafter Gang*, is amazing. He and I were close friends for nearly forty years. I actually sought him out for advice when I was a young writer. He asked me, "Do you write regularly?" Yes. "Have you sold anything?" Yes. "Then why in hell are you asking me for advice? Keep doing it." Only writing advice I ever had (except a bit from Bill Nolan).

Neal was like family. I remember him being amazed that we didn't care for the beach. He and his wife Ruth loved it. He felt our children were being deprived. One day the mail came. Opened the envelope. It was full of beach sand and seashells. A note was included: "So your children will know."

Still have that sand. Miss Neal every day.

"Survival stuff." I like that. You are writer-in-residence at Stephen F. Austin University. Does this mean you never have to leave the house, except for MoonPies?

I do leave the house to teach one long night a week, but I like it. I haven't taught lately, though. I've been traveling a lot, and I've gotten to the point where I can't stand to grade a paper. I may teach some more, but right now I'm investing that time in other projects.

Martial Arts Hall of Fame? Who do you have to whip to get in?

You have to have made a significant contribution. There are lower-level awards for Sparring Champion of the Year, Instructor of the Year, and so forth. The ones that count are the Lifetime awards, or System Creation awards. I have a little of all those from the International Martial Arts Hall of Fame, and the United States Hall of Fame. Also had one for using martial arts in my writing from the Texas Martial Arts Hall of Fame, but that hall has closed down. Too many cows in the hallway, I guess.

I love martial arts. These recognitions are nice, but it's the art itself I love, and for me, when you get right down to it, there is only one martial art—Martial Arts.

It says in your bio that you live in Texas with your wife, dog, and two cats. Is that her real name or a nickname? Do the cats get along?

Ha. I am actually known as Dog to my wife and a few friends, and she is known as Bear. Our kids are of mixed animal genetics, I suppose. Little Dog and Red Panda, and we think the Red Panda, our daughter Kasey, might be some kind of raccoon. We have a fine family and pets. Our dog is a rescued pit bull, and our cat is old.

Love your Texas Observer *essays. How did you, a fiction writer, get involved in writing opinion pieces?*

My first sales were nonfiction, so articles weren't new to me. I've had quite a few published. I started writing for the *Texas Observer* because the editor called. He asked if I would cover a Poe exhibit at the Harry Ransom Center in Austin. I started the car, drove to Austin, saw the exhibit, and wrote a piece on Poe. They liked it, and so did I (it's included in this book), so I began to do articles for them whenever I had the chance. Then they changed editors. I did one for her, then she was gone, and then they changed editors again; I did one for him, and now they've changed editors again. So, we'll see. But so far I've written quite a few *Observer* pieces. I really enjoy doing it, especially the more nostalgic pieces.

You once said that you admire Hemingway's style but not his subject matter. What the hell does that mean?

I love the way he writes, but I could care less about killing animals for trophies. He certainly wrote about more than that, but I didn't care for that aspect much. I don't see hunting as a sport. When I was growing up it was part of how we ate. It wasn't the only thing we had going, but it was a nice supplement.

Hemingway influenced us all. I liked the fact that he had a kind of simple yet poetic style. I like his short stories the best: "The Killers," one of the finest stories in the English language; "The Battler," "Hills Like White Elephants," "The Short Happy Life of Francis Macomber," "The Snows of Kilimanjaro." I also like *The Sun Also Rises* and *A Farewell to Arms*, which is kind of a hardboiled Harlequin romance for men. *Islands in the Stream*, which many do not like, is my favorite.

Ever meet Molly Ivins? Or are there more than two liberals in Texas?

I did meet her. She was drunk at a signing at the Texas Book Festival, if I remember right. Neal Barrett Jr. was with me. I think she was hitting on Neal. She was witty and funny even in that short time.

You seem to show up on movie sets of your pictures more often than most writers. Is this because you are in disguise, or do they actually want you there?

I am given a lot of freedom and even say-so on all of the stuff of mine that has actually made it to film. I'm grateful. I think I'm so much a part of my stories that it's hard to separate me from the secondary creation of film. But I'm sure there may be others in the future who will not want me on the set. I've become involved in producing as of late, so I'm getting to spend time on the sets of other films not related to my work.

What kind of car do you drive? (I ask this of everyone.)

My wife and I have a Prius apiece.

Do you have a regular drill for writing? You know what I mean.

I get up, take the dog out (if my wife doesn't beat me to it), have coffee, read my e-mail and the *New York Times* headlines, and start writing. My deal is three to five pages, and then if I want to quit, I can. If I want to continue, I can. I rarely miss that plan. I love to write, and I'm not one of those that loves "having written" (like Dorothy Parker). I love doing it. I write five to seven days a week, about three hours a day most days, though once in a while I'll come back after lunch and work a little; but mostly it's just mornings. I show up and write, polish as I go, then give it a once-over when done. Day in, day out. For my birthday I write as a treat to myself, same for Christmas and other holidays. I used to not write when I traveled, but now I do, as I travel more. I wrote mornings before the *Hap and Leonard* TV show shoots, or in the evenings when it was done. I write. That's what I do. The short time period gives me workout time, which is getting harder as I age, and time to read and be with family, watch movies, play with the dog, the usual stuff we all do. Or should do.

Did you like Winter's Bone? *Know how to skin a squirrel?*

Winter's Bone. Loved book and the film, but they don't know from squirrels. You don't clean a goddamn squirrel by hacking it. You peel its suit off, from feet to head, and then you cut the head off, and then the paws, and then you gut from stomach down, not stomach up, so as not to drag squirrel shit back up into the body. That's how you clean a squirrel.

When I was young, I ate a lot of squirrels that we hunted. My dad told me once that if I started to enjoy seeing them fall, I needed to sit down and have a serious talk with myself. We ate for food, not sport.

What do Hap and Leonard never ever talk about?

They never talk about you. Or me either.

You weren't an English major, but you seem well read in the "mainstream" classics. What do you read these days for fun?

I read what interests me and always did. I love to read history as well as fiction. I tried to read all the classics, American and otherwise, to have some understanding of how literature developed. Some I loved, some I didn't. I read classics in the genres, science fiction, historical, coming of age, fantasy, mystery, crime, suspense, western, you name it. I read the foundations for movements, like the Beats, and so on.

So many writers I can read and in five minutes realize they don't have any history. You have to know what's gone before, know the rules in order to break them. I am sometimes embarrassed for the people teaching literature. You talk to many of them and realize they have only read the modern stuff, which is fine, but the other is important too. I read modern literature if it's something that appeals or seems impactful. Same with films, art, comics, etc. One way to stay fresh is to constantly add fresh ingredients, otherwise your soup grows stale.

If you got tossed out of Texas, where would you live?

That's a toughie. I love Italy, but for long term, I'd need the USA. I like trees, but I don't like cold. Maybe Santa Fe, though I'd get tired of all that open space pretty damn quick. It would have to be someplace in the country. We live on ten acres of woods with a pond now, and we love it.

I do love Texas, though its warts are many and its sublime moments are few (except for us). We have peace and quiet and good people around, even if some of them love Jesus insanely and vote Republican.

Shit, you can't have everything.

I judge my neighbors on their character, actually, not on who they vote for or what mythology they serve. If they can rise above those things on a daily basis, and if I can rise above my own prejudices, then it's fine. Of course, they're wrong and I'm right.

Okra question: boiled or fried?

Pickled.

DARK INSPIRATION

I CAN'T THINK ABOUT Edgar Allan Poe without thinking about my life, because he was there in dark spirit, in my room and in my head. He was out there in the shadows of the East Texas pines, roaming along the creeks and the Sabine River, a friendly specter with gothic tales to tell. It was a perfect place for him. East Texas. It's the part of Texas that is behind the pine curtain, down here in the damp dark. It's Poe country, hands down.

These thoughts were in my mind as I toured the Harry Ransom Center's current exhibition, *From Out That Shadow: The Life and Legacy of Edgar Allan Poe*. The Center, at the University of Texas at Austin, is celebrating the bicentennial of Poe's birth with an exhibition that includes original manuscripts and illustrations. Looking at these artifacts, it occurred to me that Poe reached out from the grave and saved this East Texan from the aluminum chair factory. I know there are those who will say working in an aluminum chair factory is good honest work, and I'm going to agree. But I will say without hesitation and with no concern of insult that it damn sure wasn't work of my choosing, and that it takes the skill of a trained raccoon and the IQ of a can of green beans, minus the label, to get it done.

Like Sisyphus forever rolling his rock uphill, I feared I would spend my time on earth matching up aluminum runners, or linking chain to be pinned together by hissing and snapping and cutting and crimping machines, which in turn would be forklifted away in shiny piles of bent rods and flexible seats. Something to be sold and brought out on hot days at barbecues, and on hot nights to give mosquito-attacked, beer-drinking drive-in theater patrons a place for their butts to nestle.

I did all manner of work after that, some of it even less pleasant, actually, but it was that factory, the trapped tedium and uniformity of it all, that has stayed with me like a scar. Again, it's good honest work like digging a ditch or filling condom machines in gas stations, but even to this day, I have bad dreams of the aluminum chair factory, like some kind of horrid, slinking, saliva-dripping imp, clanging and cutting and crimping, and tugging at my soul. When it tugs, I can feel my spirit move inside my head. I feel it being slowly drawn away, and I awake thinking my life as a writer has all been a dream. That now it's time for me to get up and pull on my clothes and go to work and make lawn furniture.

But it's only a dream, because Poe, bless his little crazy heart and messed-up mind, like some kind of superhero came to save me. Climbed up out of the grave and swooped out from the darkness and stuck his shadow in my head and gave me something to hide beneath and something to investigate.

His shadow had been with me before, when I was kid, but during my time in the factory I had lost it for a while. When it came back, it came back with a dark, wing-flapping vengeance, and brothers and sisters, glory hallelujah, as the church folks say, I was set free.

Let me explain.

When I was a boy growing up in East Texas, from first grade to fifth, I lived in a town with about a hundred people. It was a fun thing for a child in many ways. I lived a kind of Huck Finn existence, except I got to go home to a loving family when I tired of the woods and creeks and bicycle rides. But without those things, I found the world where I lived somewhat empty. It was as if everything was painted gray, and there was very little shading; it was flat gray, like the walls of a prison, inside and out.

But there were little bits of hope. There were comics, bright and shiny and rich in action, all in color for a dime. And there were books, which gave me strange new worlds and all manner of adventure, and then there was Poe.

My family was a poor one. My father couldn't read or write and my mother had an eleventh-grade education, but she was a reader. And when I was a very young boy, she handed me a book of horror and detective tales by Poe.

That book darkened and shaded the gray around me, gave me velvet shadows that quivered at the bottom of my dreams. They thrilled me so deeply I often awoke with such an intense feeling of excitement and fascination that I would walk about my room for hours in an overstimulated stupor, stopping weak-kneed to grab a pen and paper to try to write down my own stories of wicked doings and dark designs. He was the first author to do that for me. There was something so strange about his work, yet so inviting and satisfying. For a long time, Poe owned me.

At the Ransom Center, I read that he liked the night and dark places. I almost let out a whoop, because I'm much the same way. I live a more balanced life, no drunken forays and drugged nights, and I like the day better than Poe, but when I write during the day, I like it dark. I like the shades drawn. I love sitting in darkness and reading with only one light on. I like rain and grim skies and an atmosphere that creeps with possibilities dark and forlorn.

Perhaps this is because I read Poe at an early age, or perhaps it was because he was a kindred spirit: someone who felt better clothed in shadows and mystery, someone who liked a world of twisted logic and bizarre puzzles, and found it more interesting than day-to-day dealings, discussions of the weather and the position of the Yankees or the Cowboys in the World Series or Super Bowl.

I'm not one of those who thinks Poe's drinking, depression, and drug use contributed to his writing and made it better. I believe he wrote to escape these personal demons. Poverty was another problem he had, another thing from which he wished to escape, and when I was a kid, and in fact until I was in my middle twenties, it was part of my daily existence as well. Sometimes, to escape the thought of pockets full of lint and no change, it was necessary to enter into a world where anything was possible. A world of one's own creation. But to do so, others had to show you how to open the doors and give you a bit of furniture here and there. They had to tease you into coming over to their side and looking around inside their house.

Writers as diverse as Kipling, Tennessee Williams, and H.P. Lovecraft, his greatest disciple, have acknowledged their debt to Poe. He moved through their writings like an apparition. His shadow is large, and it's changeable. He wrote detective stories, invented them for that matter. He wrote horror stories, and stories of the psychologically weird and the grotesque, as well as stories of dark humor. He wrote a little bit of everything, including love poems, provided you like your love dark and dank and dead.

As a person, Poe was so acidic and unpopular that even his literary executor tried to destroy his reputation. But his talent remains, vibrant and as influential as ever. Not even his literary executor could drown that. Poe may go down deep for a while, pushed there by fashion and critics, but he floats. He bobs up. He's always there to remind us of his dark genius. He may be the most influential American writer ever, and maybe one of the most influential in the world. He had such impact on the world of literature that awards are named after him, comics are drawn depicting his work, and there is even an action figure of Poe, minus the kung fu grip. Take that, Dostoevsky!

And this brings me back to the aluminum chair factory and his influence. Yeah, that's right. I'm never far away from the aluminum chair factory.

I thought of his stories while I worked, carrying rods, or racking links, or holding my foot on a pedal that made a machine hiss, thump and bind. I thought of his stories until I could hear the beating of Poe's tell-tale heart beneath my feet. See his black cat out of the corner of my eye. Imagine a wall freshly bricked up with a man scratching at it from the other side. He helped me get through my shifts. He was there, and he's here now, with me most mornings when I write. He is stronger than the aluminum chair factory. He was a fate-changer for me, and I love him for it.

Thank you, Edgar Allan Poe, for saving me from a fate that would have been a premature burial the length of my life.

Thank goodness Poe was correct when he wrote, "The boundaries which divide Life from Death are at best shadowy and vague. Who shall say where the one ends and where the other begins?"

Anyone with a creative spark knows what that means. And anyone of a creative spirit is thankful for it. It gives us a place to go that isn't contained and bound in the plain gray wrapper of our flesh.

Thank you, Edgar Allan Poe.

THE DROWNED MAN

In our early twenties, my wife and I didn't have any money or real jobs. We were going to college and doing day labor in Nacogdoches. What we didn't have was a house we owned. The one we were living in rented for very little, but it had some drawbacks. One was an outhouse. The outhouse was a favorite hangout for snakes so big they looked as if they belonged in a Tarzan movie, not to mention spiders large enough to wear multi-legged pants. Every trip to the privy became worthy of an Indiana Jones adventure.

Another drawback was no inside water. There was a pump to a well outside and a water hose, but stripping off and taking a bath with the hose in freezing weather was, to put it mildly, uncomfortable. Our heat was firewood I chopped to burn in two large fireplaces. There was a small electric heater that whined like a small child and might have blown up had we tried to warm a marshmallow in front of it.

So we wouldn't starve, we decided to move to Starrville, where my parents lived, and stay with them while we worked and Karen went to school part-time at Tyler Junior College. So in my oil-guzzling old Ford and Karen's truck, we headed out, like two leftover Joads from *The Grapes of Wrath*, and went north to Starrville, which is about the size of a postage stamp. Actually, we ended up on its outskirts, so we can't claim actual residence there.

I had given up on my university degree and decided I wanted to be a farmer. Part of this was a love for the idea and the fact I had grown up in the country around this sort of thing. My parents generally raised a garden and a few hogs and chickens, so I had experience. It was a sincere lifestyle we thought might get us through until I could write stories and novels, which was what I really wanted to do, and until Karen could get her degree in criminology-sociology, and perhaps go about harassing or rehabilitating criminals, depending on the criminal.

Neither of us saw our back-to-the-land venture as a lifetime job, but something we could enjoy in our youth, a means to an end. So we moved, and it was nice not to put out $30 a month for rent. This was the 1970s; for us, $30 was a lot of money. We had my parents' land to raise a large garden, plus a truck crop patch for vegetables to sell, and out back we had room for hogs, mules, goats, and a chicken house. We bought a mule, and I learned to plow. I bought all kinds of old equipment and went to work. My parents moved into town, probably due to our presence, and we took over the place temporarily.

The first year was successful. We were living off about $4,000, a small sum even for that time. Everything we ate, we raised. We bought only wheat berries, sugar, salt, animal feed, and a few other odds and ends. We ground the wheat berries, made our own bread and sold vegetables from the garden for an occasional splurge in Tyler on a movie or an outing at a cheap Mexican restaurant. It was pretty much a daylight-to-dark job. I didn't write as much as I thought. I kept telling myself I would. Eventually.

The second summer brought dry weather and not as much food. My wife went to work loading packages of meat into refrigerated cars, the contents to be delivered to convenience stores, and I got a job working the rose fields. There I worked with other poor folk. When winter came, there was less work, so fewer of us were kept on. I was glad to be among those kept for rose-digging time. They dug the roses with a machine, and we tossed them into trucks that hauled them to be loaded into refrigeration cars. The roses, fresh from the ground and dangling lots of wet dirt, were heavy, cumbersome, and prickly. It was a job that, once started, had to be finished, so we were literally working day and night, sometimes loading roses by spotlight.

One night after work, the wind shifted, and the rain thumped our roof like a thug with a cat o' nine tails. When I went outside for a look, the porch light made everything look like something Noah might have spied from the poop deck of the ark. Lots of water. When morning came, the storm was gone and the high water had drained out, but the ground was wet and icy, and the sky was the color of pearl.

My boss lived close by, and it became his ritual during rose-digging to pick me up at my house and drive me to and from the fields. On this morning, we crossed a little bridge, and as we did, we both spied off to our right, down on the creek bank, a large box. My boss said, "I think that's a toolbox." He pulled over, and we went down for a look. Sure enough, it was a toolbox, the kind that goes in the back of a pickup. As if on command, we turned our heads and glanced under the bridge. On the other side, we could see a pickup with its nose in the creek. We went over and discovered that not only was there a truck, but there was a man behind the wheel. He was swollen from the water, and his flesh looked puffy and soft, like bread dough. He reminded me of a horror version of the Pillsbury Doughboy, his eyes swollen shut, his lips like two fat, dark worms. My boss said, "I think I know him."

We decided that most likely he had driven across the bridge when the water was high and had been swept into the creek. We drove to a phone (no cell phones then) and called authorities. That night, I dreamed of that poor man, and the thing that came to me was not only is life short, but quit screwing around; our time is brief, and nothing is promised. It's what you do now that matters, not what you do tomorrow or what you think you will do tomorrow.

We finished the rose field job as the weather turned worse, and for three months I didn't have a job. My wife, always my greatest supporter, insisted she continue working and that I should write until the end of the year, when the weather broke. I think she knew how bad I wanted to do it, and how mortal I felt after the discovery of that dead man. I set to work, and since I didn't know what I was doing, I wrote a short story a day for ninety days. I sent them out, one after another, and they sent them back. There were a lot of markets then.

Eventually I collected around a thousand rejects on those 90 stories. But I felt I was in the game, and learning.

We abandoned our farming venture, moved back to Nacogdoches. I got a janitor job at the university, and my wife got her degree. My job started midafternoon, so in the mornings I wrote, and when I got off work I wrote or read for another hour or two. Gradually, I began to sell a lot of stories and novels and went full-time as a writer and a house dad.

I think I would have written eventually. I had already sold a few articles. But when I saw the Drowned Man, I realized that if I wasn't careful, I could end up working my life away, always planning on writing and never seriously pursuing it; that at the end of my life, I might end up with a fraction of the work I could have done, writing now and then while doing a job I didn't really like.

It was a sad way of finding my eureka moment, but here I am, more than thirty-five years later, and instead of the smattering of stories I might have written, the Drowned Man pushed me forward, gave me will and placed the cold hand of mortality on my shoulder. I've become comfortable with it resting there. I think of it as a gentle reminder not to waste my time on earth—and not only with the writing, but with family, with all the things that matter.

I know it's odd, and I don't even know the poor man's name. But in a strange way, I owe him a lot.

DARKNESS IN THE EAST

NOIR IS A FRENCH word meaning dark. It's used to identify a certain type of grim fiction or film. Don't let the French name fool you. There's plenty of noir right here in East Texas, though it's mixed with southern gothic and western and all manner of stuff; it's a gumbo boiled in hell. I know. I'm from East Texas. I've seen it. I've written about it. Weird as some of it is, fictionalized as the work is, it comes from a wellspring of true events you just can't make up.

Let's clear up one thing. There are plenty of good people in East Texas (saw one yesterday), but if you're a writer of crime fiction, which I am at least some of the time, you're not looking for good people. You're looking for weirdos, criminals, malcontents, and the just plain stupid. That's your meat if you write crime.

In spite of the word, not all of the fiction or films associated with this genre are completely dark. Noir wears many hats, some even with bright feathers in them. Sometimes noir can laugh, which is where I come in. It's where East Texas comes in. You can't point at noir and call it one thing, but it usually has some of these elements: existentialist attitude, cynical and desperate characters, wise-ass talk, rain and shadows, a lightning bolt and shadowed blinds, sweaty sheets and cigarette smoke, whiskey breath and dark street corners where shots are fired and a body is found, and long black cars squealing tires as they race around poorly lit corners.

For me as a writer, noir takes place in the backwoods and slick, brick streets and red clay roads and sandy hills of East Texas. My noir is about Baptist preachers claiming with lilting poetry to be called by the Lord to preach The Word, but who have intentions as false as a stuffed sock in a rock star's pants; pretty soon they're gone with the congregation's money and three deacon's wives are knocked up. My noir is about the deep backwoods and small-town girls with inflated dreams and big blonde hair and the kind of oozing sex appeal that would make a good family man set fire to the wife's cat and use it as a torch to burn down his house—with his wife in it.

You got your slicked-back-shiny-haired used car salesman with more better deals and a plan to burn his business for the insurance money. You got your muscle-armed, pot-bellied hick with a toothpick and a John Deere gimme cap, forever dressed in hunting boots, camouflage pants and a wife-beater T-shirt—even if his destination is just the barber shop or the barbecue joint. He's the kind of guy who likes to get drunk every night and drive home weaving. He's the kind of guy whose last words are to his best buddy in the passenger seat—"Hey, hold my beer and watch this"—and who then proceeds to unzip his pants and attempt to drive his truck with his manly appendage.

You got this same kind of guy at the Wednesday prayer meeting, wearing a concealed-carry pistol tucked under his worn-out high-school letter jacket in case the Muslims attack or there's an unexpected run on grape juice and tasteless wafers by liberal Democrats. He's the kind of guy who carries a pack of condoms in his front pocket to signify high hopes for the big-breasted, blonde church organist with an orthodontist's grin and an ass like two volley balls banging together in a croaker sack. If that don't happen, well hell, on his way home he's got a spotlight and a rifle in the trunk for popping blinded rabbits. In fact, in that trunk he's got so many guns that his guns own guns, and who knows where that kind of firepower might lead? For example, there are those guys down at the job who done him wrong, the ex-wife that got the kids, the dog that digs in his yard, and all those folks who want the new health care program so they can pull the plug on Grandma. They could all get a taste of his ammunition if the mood strikes him right.

You got the Aryan Nations with their pale skins covered in jailhouse tattoos, crosses and swastikas, a heart with Mama written across it on a crawling snake, their necks so covered in tattoo print they look like they fell asleep on a damp newspaper, talking authoritatively with tears in their eyes about the Bible they've never read, cussing science and manmade books.

Then you got the Dixie flag, southern heritage guys talking about how fine it would be had the South won the war, worrying that they're losing their white heritage, which when you get right down to it is most likely great-grandpa's weed-infested grave, a mayonnaise sandwich on white bread, a MoonPie, a bag of pork skins, a big Bud Light, and a Jim Beam chaser. Here in East Texas, we got rampaging horse-shooters, wife-beaters, child abusers, murderers, gangs (yeah, really), scripture-quoting psychopaths and enough crystal meth that if some cooker gets drunk and drops a match, he could blow us all the way to Mars.

The people I write about lurk in small East Texas towns, living in same-alike houses, on cleared clay lots with little anemic bushes in their yards, yards that often sport mossy gnomes and colorful wooden frames painted up like bent-over grannies. In the backyard, the flowers may even be holding down that missing relative not seen since 1985, or the freezer might contain a human head next to a plastic bag of hotdogs.

Let's come back to this, as it might save me from a lynching. Yes, East Texas is full of good people. Some of them might even be Christians. Some might be used car salesmen and back-road runners wearing camouflage with a toothpick in their mouth. They might be public servants so paranoid they want college students to be armed in the case of a nut going wild; students could kill the nut and each other in a crossfire, but these are otherwise good people with the best of intentions. Not everyone is out to do bad. Some have done well with their GEDs, and they have a nice library—consisting primarily of *Guns and Ammo* magazines, and others where naked women wear only staples. Seriously, I even know one person who has been to clown college—and graduated. These are my peeps, man.

Sometimes you look at noir and realize it's real, not just a story or a film. Some of it is so like a sucking gunshot wound that, to keep from hanging yourself from a shower rod, you have to laugh at it, make fun of it. You got to do what fire-fighters and policemen do—and when I speak of the latter I don't mean senselessly beating a suspect with three feet of water hose and a telephone book. I mean laugh at the terrible things, because laughter is the only antidote. It's the eight-hundred-pound gorilla that holds the dark at bay.

My noir may not be your noir, but nonetheless it is noir, and though it's not all I write, it's a lot of what I write. It often informs work of mine that I meant to be absolutely as far away from noir as I'd like to be from the Tea Party. East Texas has its own kind of dark side that comes deep-fried, baptized, and sanctified with a side of hollow points and racial epithets. That's my beat, here in the shadows and sticky heat, nestled up tight as a hungry chigger in a fat man's armpit.

When you write crime, you're not looking at the good that exists. You're thinking about and looking at the bad, at the criminals, at the lowlifes and how they affect those who just want to do their part—people who just want to go to their jobs, raise their families, and maybe retire with a lakefront view and a good supply of adult diapers, with no one cooking crystal meth next door or kicking in the door to take their plasma television or sell their crippled dog to medical research.

Those bad folks are out there, like the flu. Waiting. They are outnumbered by the good, but all it takes is one bad sucker to ruin your day. We all know that therein lies the appeal of the noir tale, the books of mystery and suspense, crime and sacrifice, trips to the Dairy Queen gone horribly wrong. Stories like that are a way to flirt with the dark without having to actually date and marry it.

We know bad can happen, but mostly we like to think we're pretty safe in our bedrooms at night with books in our hands. We can turn the pages and see what happens, or we can put it down, turn off the light, and go to sleep. On some level, it's like an inoculation against disaster, pre-coping with things that might happen and probably never will, a metaphorical way of dealing with the Big D. And I don't mean Dallas.

That part will happen. Be it by crime, poorly chewed steak lodged in the windpipe, car wreck, or lying in an old folks' home wired up like a spaceman watching shadows move across the wall. Noir is our way of saying howdy to the dark side without going there to live.

At least not yet.

DOGGONE JUSTICE

Things have changed. The world has evolved. A punch in the mouth ain't what it used to be.

Once you were more apt to settle your own problems, or have them settled for you, by an angry party. Teeth could be lost, and bones could be broken, but mostly you just got a black eye, a bloody nose, or you might be found temporarily unconscious, face down in a small pool of blood out back of a bar with a shoe missing.

These days, even defending yourself can be tricky. It seems to me a butt-whipping in the name of justice has mutated to three shots from an automatic weapon at close quarters and three frames of bowling with your dead head. There are too many nuts with guns these days, and most of them just think the other guy is nuts. An armed society is a polite society only if those armed are polite. Otherwise, it just makes a fellow nervous.

Still, not wishing back the past. Not exactly. But there are elements of the past I do miss. There are times when I like the idea of settling your own hash—without gunfire. Sometimes the other guy has it coming.

When I was a kid in East Texas, we lived in a home that sat on a hill overlooking what was called a beer joint or honky-tonk. Beyond the tonk was a highway, and beyond that a drive-in theater standing as tall and white as a monstrous slice of Wonder Bread.

You could see the drive-in from our house, and from that hill my mother and I would watch the drive-in without sound. What I remember best were Warner Bros. cartoons. As we watched, mom would tell me what the cartoon characters were saying. Later, when I saw the cartoons on TV—something we didn't have at the time—I was shocked to discover Mom had made up the stories out of the visuals. My mom was a dad-burned liar. It was an early introduction to storytelling.

But this isn't storytelling. This is reporting, and what I'm about to tell you is real, and I was there. It's one of my first memories. So mixed up was the memory that, years later, when I was a grown man, I had to ask my mother if it was a dream, or fragments of memories shoved together. I had some things out of order, and I had mixed in an item or two, but my mother sorted them out for me. This is what happened.

My mother and I stayed at home nights while my dad was on the road, working on trucks. He was a mechanic and a troubleshooter for a truck company. My entertainment was my mother and that silent drive-in and the fistfights that sometimes occurred in the honky-tonk parking lot, along with the colorful language I filed away for later use.

We were so poor that my dad used to say that if it cost a quarter to crap, we'd have to throw up. There wasn't money for a lot of toys, nor at that time a TV, which was a fairly newfangled instrument anyway. We listened to the radio when the tubes finally glowed and warmed up enough for us to bring in something.

Dad decided that the drive-in, seen through a window at a great distance, and a static-laden radio with a loose tube that if touched incorrectly would knock you across the room with a flash of light and a hiss like a spitting cobra, were not proper things for a growing boy. He thought I needed a friend.

Below, at the tonk, a dog delivered pups. Dad got me one. It was a small, fuzzy ball of dynamite. Dad named him Honky-Tonk. I called him Blackie. I loved that dog so dearly that even writing about him now makes me emotional. We were like brothers. We drank out of the same bowl, when mom didn't catch us; and he slept in my bed, and we shared fleas. We had a large place to play, a small creek out back, and beyond that a junkyard of rusting cars full of broken glass and sharp metal and plenty of tetanus.

And there was the house.

It sat on a hill above the creek, higher than our house, surrounded by glowing red and yellow flowers immersed in dark beds of dirt. It was a beautiful sight, and on a fine spring day those flowers pulled me across that little creek and straight to them as surely as a siren calling to a mariner. Blackie came with me, tongue hanging out, his tail wagging. Life was great. We were as happy as if we had good sense and someone else's money.

I went up there to look, and Blackie, like any self-respecting dog, went there to dig in the flowerbed. I was watching him do it, probably about to join in, when the door opened and a big man came out and snatched my puppy up by the hind legs and hit him across the back of the head with a pipe, or stick, and then, as if my dog were nothing more than a used condom, tossed him into the creek.

Then the man looked at me.

I figured I was next and bolted down the hill and across the creek to tell my mother. She had to use the next-door neighbor's phone, as this was long before everyone had one in their pocket. It seemed no sooner than she walked back home from making her call than my dad arrived like Mr. Death in our old black car.

He got out wearing greasy work clothes and told me to stay and started toward the House of Flowers. I didn't stay. I was devastated. I had been crying so hard my mother said I hiccupped when I breathed. I had to see what was about to happen. Dad went across the creek and to the back door and knocked gently, like a Girl Scout selling cookies. The door opened, and there was the Flower Man.

My dad hit him. It was a quick, straight punch and fast as a bee flies. Flower Man went down faster than a duck on a june bug, but without the satisfaction. He was out. He was hit so hard his ancestors in the prehistoric past fell out of a tree.

Dad grabbed him by the ankles and slung him through the flowerbed like a dull weed-eater, mowed down all those flowers, even made a mess of the dirt. If Flower Man came awake during this process, he didn't let on. He knew it was best just to let Dad finish. It was a little bit like when a grizzly bear gets you; you just kind of have to go with it. When the flowers were flat, Dad swung the man by his ankles like a discus, and we watched him sail out and into the shallow creek with a sound akin to someone dropping wet laundry on cement.

We went down in the creek and found Blackie. He was still alive. Flower Man didn't move. He lay in the shallow water and was at that moment as much a part of that creek as the gravel at its bottom.

Daddy took Blackie home and treated his wound, a good knock on the noggin, and that dog survived until the age of thirteen. When I was eighteen, Blackie and I were standing on the edge of the porch watching the sun go down, and Blackie went stiff, flopped over the edge, dead for real this time.

Bless my daddy. We had our differences when I was growing up, and we didn't see eye to eye on many things. But he was my hero from that day after. Hardly a day goes by that I don't remember what he did that day, and how he made something so dark and dismal turn bright.

No one sued. Then, events like that were considered personal. To pull a lawyer into it was not only embarrassing but just plain sissy. Today we'd be sued for the damage my dog did, the damage my dad did, and emotional distress, not to mention bandages and the laundry bill for the wet and dirty clothes.

I know the man loved his flowers. I know my dog did wrong, if not bad. I know I didn't give a damn at the time and thought about digging there myself. But I was a kid and Blackie was a pup, and if ever there was a little East Texas homespun justice delivered via a fast arm and a hard fist, that was it.

Flower Man, not long after that, moved away, slunk off like a carnival that owed bills. A little later we moved as well, shortly after the drive-in was wadded up by a tornado. That's another story.

THE DAY BEFORE THE DAY AFTER

I WAS FIVE YEARS old, and I lived in a house on top of a hill. Below it was a honky-tonk, and a highway ran in front of that. Across the highway was a drive-in theater. There were a few houses nearby, and there was a junkyard. This and my parents and my little black dog were my world.

It was the 1950s, a time when our country feared the Russians and feared the Bomb. We were the first generation to grow up under the shadow of the Bomb, and it was a big Bomb, and from comic books and B movies we knew that if it were dropped we'd be knocked ass over teakettle, and that when the smoke cleared there would be nothing but radioactive bones left, except for those lucky few who could afford bomb shelters and plenty of canned goods and drinking water. Sometimes the builders forgot about toilets down there, but at the End of the World you can't have everything.

Of course, even if one did survive in a bomb shelter, then, as the B movies depicted, once the survivors were brave enough to come out of their holes and venture into the light of a new, bleak world, there would be that pesky problem of radiation, and, of course, giant lizards or ants or some guy with three eyes and a limp who wanted nothing better than to eat you and build a hut from your hair and bones.

We believed that then—that, overnight, radiation could create critters that had never before existed and swell common household rodents and lizards and insects to giant size.

I mention all this because a neighbor was building a shelter in his back yard, a deep hole in the ground where things could be stored in case of a nuclear attack. I don't remember much about the building of it, but I remember my parents talking about it. Their conversation went something like this.

Mom: "He'll be safe and we won't." Dad: "It'll fill up with water." Mom: "What if the Russians drop the Bomb?" Me: "What Bomb? What's a Russian?" Mom: "Don't worry about it, Joey. Russians are people. They are evil communists who live on the other side of the world." Me: "What's a communist? How do they live on the other side of the world? Won't they fall off?" Mom: "It's okay, Joey. Don't worry about it." Dad: "Russians drop the Damn Bomb, you can bend over and kiss your ass goodbye." Me: "Bomb?" Mom: "It's okay, Joey. No one is going to drop the Bomb." Mom to Dad: "He'll be safe down there and we won't, and we have Joey to think about." Me: "Bomb?" Mom: "We'll be fine, Joey." Dad: "I tell you, the son of a bitch'll fill up with water."

And so it went.

There I was, an imaginative and, dare I say it, precocious little kid, and I had that Damn Bomb to worry about, and believe me, I did worry. But the idea of it was kind of cool too, because if a bomb was dropped, and I got under the bed with my dog and survived—because it was pretty safe down there—I could come up and live in an exciting world with radioactive lizards and a lot of abandoned stores with candy bars in them.

I thought it made perfect sense.

But here we were, waiting on the Bomb, and one day my dad was at work and Mom and I were home with my dog, and the sky turned green. No joke. Green. At least that's how I remember it. I also remember that my mom suddenly went quiet, an unusual thing, because she was usually entertaining me with stories, or talking to herself and answering, so when she turned silent I knew something was wrong.

Green sky. Quiet mother. Oh, my goodness, I thought. It's the Damn Bomb. In less than a day radioactive lizards would be tramping over our back yard and licking clean our busted mayonnaise jars and nosing through my comic books.

Mom went about opening all the windows in the house, even the doors to the outside. The air was as still as an oil painting and felt heavy as a wet blanket. There was no sound. No birds were chirping. Not even blue jays, and they never shut up. You had the impression even a frog feared to fart.

Mom kept staring out the window, and then I saw what she was staring at: a big black cloud, and there was a little piece of it hanging down like a fish hook, near the drive-in theater screen, and then the hook extended and started toward the ground. Then came a sound like a freight train and it was as if an invisible hand reached down and wadded up that screen like a piece of aluminum foil. My mother snatched my hand, and we were out the door and she was dragging me across the yard toward the neighbor's house, the one with the bomb shelter. My little dog, Blackie, was hot on our heels.

I thought: I have seen the Damn Bomb, and it's a big black cloud that wads up things. The neighbor met us halfway, as he was on his way to get us, thank goodness, and we ran with him toward the shelter.

I doubt that at this point I was thinking about getting under the bed, radioactive lizards, or free candy bars. But even to this day I remember being scared. I remember all four of us, three humans and a dog, running for that shelter, and then the trapdoor was opening and we went down some steps and sat on them, halfway between the bottom step and the trapdoor, me clutching my dog to my chest.

The trap was closed, and it was dark down there, and the train I had heard moments before was immediately running right over us, there in the dark. The neighbor pulled a cord, and there was light, powered by I know not what. In that light I saw shelves full of canned goods, and by canned goods I mean jars full of self-preserved foods. I seem to remember other people there, probably his family, but that's a dim memory. What I mostly remember is this: The shelter was ankle-deep in water, and there was a snake swimming in the water.

Someone screamed. The neighbor took hold of something and splashed about in that water and chased that snake all over the place, whacked at it like a madman. Then the light went out.

The train rumbled and the ground shook and the trapdoor trembled like an old man with palsy. I remember thinking maybe the lizards were up there, and maybe the Russians. I envisioned the Russians with one big eye in the middle of their foreheads, and the word, Russian, was to my young mind a key to their comic-book abilities. And then the great lizard, train, Russians, whatever, passed, and there was silence.

A light eventually came on. Maybe the light inside the shelter, or maybe the light from the open trapdoor, but the next thing I remember was seeing that dead snake on the bottom step of the wooden stairs, and all that water.

Out in the light, we looked toward the drive-in. It was gone, of course, and the honky-tonk was missing its roof. Pieces of this and that were scattered all about.

And our house?

Wasn't touched. Neither was the neighbor's house. The tornado had come and gone, jumping over our homes like a cloudy kangaroo, leaving us with nothing more than a fearful memory and stained underwear.

I learned several things that day, and I have taken them all to heart.

First: The world is an uncertain place. One moment you can be slapping sandwich meat on bread, and the next moment they can find your ass in a ditch.

The second was that if a tornado scared me that bad, maybe being a survivor after the Damn Bomb had been dropped might not be as exciting as I thought.

And most important I knew this: As Dad had said, if you build a bomb shelter, root cellar, or storm shelter in East Texas, the son of a bitch will fill up with water.

Oh yeah, one thing Dad didn't think about. Sometimes a snake, no matter how tight you think you've built things, will get down there with you, and the lights might go out.

BIBLIOGRAPHY
(A work in progress)

"Hap Collins and Leonard Pine" mysteries

Savage Season, 1990

Mucho Mojo, 1994

Two-Bear Mambo, 1995

Bad Chili, 1997

Rumble Tumble, 1998

Veil's Visit, 1999 (includes the eponymous story, written with
    Andrew Vachss)

Captains Outrageous, 2001

Vanilla Ride, 2009

Hyenas, 2011 (a novella)

Devil Red, 2011

Dead Aim, 2013 (a novella)

The "Drive-In" series

*The Drive-In: A "B" Movie with Blood and Popcorn, Made in
    Texas*, 1988

The Drive-In 2: Not Just One of Them Sequels, 1989

The Drive-In: A Double-Feature, 1997 (omnibus compiling
  the first two)

The Drive-In: The Bus Tour, 2005

The "Ned the Seal" trilogy

Zeppelins West, 2001

Flaming London, 2006

Flaming Zeppelins: The Adventures of Ned the Seal, 2010

Other novels

Act of Love, 1980

Texas Night Riders, 1983 (originally published under the
  pseudonym Ray Slater)

Dead in the West, 1986 (written in 1980)

Magic Wagon, 1986

The Nightrunners, 1987 (written in 1982 as *Night of the
  Goblins*)

Cold in July, 1989

Tarzan: The Lost Adventure, 1995 (with Edgar Rice
  Burroughs)

The Boar, 1998 (initially a limited edition, later republished)

Freezer Burn, 1999

Waltz of Shadows, 1999 (written in 1991)

Something Lumber This Way Comes, 1999 (children's book)

The Big Blow, 2000

Blood Dance, 2000 (written in the early '80s)

The Bottoms, 2000
A Fine Dark Line, 2002
Sunset and Sawdust, 2004
Lost Echoes, 2007
Leather Maiden, 2008
Under the Warrior Sun, 2010
All the Earth, Thrown to the Sky, 2011
Edge of Dark Water, 2012
In Waders from Mars, 2012 (children's book)
The Thicket, 2013
Hot in December, 2013

Screenplays collected

Shadows West, 2012
The Nightrunners, 2012 (with Neal Barrett Jr., in *Written with a Razor: Short Stories and a Screenplay*)

Mark Stone: MIA Hunter series

These are a few novels Lansdale wrote under the pseudonym Jack Buchanan, probably cowritten with Stephen Mertz. Some people erroneously report that Lansdale is responsible for the entire series, which is definitely not true.

Hanoi Deathgrip (Stone: MIA Hunter #3)
Mountain Massacre (Stone: MIA Hunter #4)
Saigon Slaughter (the consensus seems to be that this is #7, though some claim #8)

SHORT STORIES

Collections

By Bizarre Hands, 1989

Stories by Mama Lansdale's Youngest Boy, 1991 (aka *Author's Choice Monthly* #18)

Bestsellers Guaranteed, 1993

Electric Gumbo: A Lansdale Reader, 1994 (Quality Paperback Book Club exclusive)

Writer of the Purple Rage, 1994

A Fist Full of Stories (and Articles), 1996

The Good, the Bad, and the Indifferent, 1997

Private Eye Action, As You Like It, 1998 (with Lewis Shiner)

Triple Feature, 1999

The Long Ones: Nuthin' but Novellas, 2000

High Cotton, 2000

For a Few Stories More, 2002 (limited edition "Lost Lansdale" vol. 4; the "ultra-limited" edition of this book included a previously unpublished young adult vampire novel titled *Shadow Time*, which has not appeared anywhere else)

A Little Green Book of Monster Stories, 2003

Bumper Crop, 2004

Mad Dog Summer and Other Stories, 2004 (initially a limited edition, reissued in paperback)

The King and Other Stories, 2005

God of the Razor and Other Stories, 2007

The Shadows, Kith and Kin, 2007

Sanctified and Chicken-Fried: The Portable Lansdale, 2009
Unchained and Unhinged, 2009
The Best of Joe R. Lansdale, 2010
By Bizarre Hands Rides Again, 2010
Deadman's Road, 2010
Trapped in the Saturday Matinee, 2012
Bleeding Shadows, 2013
Deadman's Crossing, 2013

Chapbooks

On the Far Side of the Cadillac Desert with Dead Folks, 1991
The Steel Valentine, 1991 (Pulphouse Hardback Magazine #7)
Steppin' Out, Summer '68, 1992
God of the Razor, 1992
Tight Little Stitches in a Dead Man's Back, 1992
Mister Weed-Eater, 1993
My Dead Dog Bobby, 1995
Bubba Ho-Tep, 2003 (novella, published standalone as a
    movie tie-in)
Duck Footed, 2005 (novella)
Christmas with the Dead, 2010 (novella)
The Cases of Dana Roberts, 2011
The Ape Man's Brother, 2012 (novella)

Uncollected Short Stories

"Castle of Shadows" from *Weirdbook* #21, 1985 (with Ardath
    Mayhar)

"Boo Yourself!" from *Whispers VI*, 1987 (ed. Stuart David
    Schiff; republished in *100 Tiny Tales of Terror*, ed.
    Martin H. Greenberg)
"Dead in the West: Screenplay," from *Screamplays*, 1997
"Disaster Club," from *Cemetery Dance* #32, 1999
"Bullets and Fire," 2011

COMIC BOOK–RELATED WRITINGS

Novels and stories with Batman

Batman: Captured by the Engines, 1991 (novel)
Batman: Terror on the High Skies, 1992 (junior novel;
    illustrated by Edward Hannigan and Dick Giordano)
"Belly Laugh, or The Joker's Trick or Treat," short story
    in *The Further Adventures of the Joker*, ed. Martin
    H. Greenberg, 1989 (reprinted in *Adventures of the
    Batman*, ed. Greenberg, 1995)
"Subway Jack," short story in *The Further Adventures of
    Batman*, ed. Greenberg, 1989 (features Lansdale's
    character the God of the Razor, reprinted in *Tales of the
    Batman*, ed. Greenberg, 1994)

Graphic novels and comic books

Lone Ranger & Tonto, 1993, 4 issues and trade paperback (art
    by Tim Truman and Rick Magyar)
Jonah Hex: Two-Gun Mojo, 1993, 5 issues, and 2014 trade
    paperback (art by Tim Truman)

Jonah Hex: Riders of the Worm and Such, 1995, 5 issues (art by Tim Truman)

Blood and Shadows, 1996, 4 issues (art by Mark A. Nelson)

The Spirit: The New Adventures #8, 1998 (art by John Lucas)

Red Range, 1999 (art by Sam Glanzman)

Jonah Hex: Shadows West, 1999, 3 issues (art by Tim Truman)

Conan and the Songs of the Dead, 2006, 5 issues, and 2007 paperback (art by Tim Truman)

Marvel Adventures: Fantastic Four #32, Jan. 2008 (art by Ronan Cliquet)

Pigeons from Hell, 2008 (adaptation of the Robert E. Howard short story; art by Nathan Fox)

Yours Truly, Jack the Ripper, 2010, 3 issues (with John L. Lansdale; art by Kevin Colden)

30 Days of Night: Night, Again, 2011, 4 issues and trade paperback (art by Sam Kieth)

H.P. Lovecraft's The Dunwich Horror, 2011, 4 issues (art by Peter Bergting)

That Hell-Bound Train, 2011, 3 issues (with John L. Lansdale, based on a story by Robert Bloch; art by Dave Wachter)

Crawling Sky, 2013 (with Keith Lansdale and Brian Denham)

Short stories

Drive-By, 1993 (adapted from a story by Andrew Vachss; art by Gary Gianni; originally published in Andrew Vachss, *Hard Looks* #5; reprinted in Andrew Vachss,

Hard Looks and as a limited-edition trade paperback
containing Vachss's original story, Lansdale's comic
script, and the as-published illustrated story)

"Grease Trap" in *Creature Features*, 1994 (art by Ted Naifeh)

"Shootout at Ice Flats" in *Supergirl Annual* #1, 1996 (with
Neal Barrett Jr.; art by Robert Branishi and Stan Woch)

"The Elopement" in *Weird War Tales* #2 (of 4), July 1997 (art
by Sam Glanzman, DC)

"The Initiation" in *Gangland* #4 (of 4), Sept. 1998 (with
Rick Klaw; art by Tony Salmons)

"Betrothed" in *Flinch* #5, Oct. 1999 (art by Rick Burchett,
DC/Vertigo)

"The Split" in *Strange Adventures* #3 (of 4), Jan. 2000 (art by
Richard Corben)

"Red Romance" in *Flinch* #11, May 2000

"Brer Hoodoo" in *Flinch* #13, July 2000 (art by Tim
Truman)

"Devil's Sombrero" in *Weird Western Tales* #2 (of 4), May 2001

"Steam Rider: The Steam-Powered Heart" in *Amazing
Fantasy* #20, June 2006

"Mice and Money" in *Marvel Romance Redux* #5 (subtitle
"Love Is a Four Letter Word"), June 2006 (reprinted in
Mighty Marvel Romance paperback)

"Gunhawk: Midnight Gun" in *Strange Westerns Starring the
Black Rider*, Aug. 2006 (art by Rafa Garres); reprinted
in *Mighty Marvel Westerns* hardcover

"Moonlight Sonata" in *Tales from the Crypt* #7, Aug. 2008
(art by Chris Noeth)

Adaptations of previously published stories, by Lansdale unless noted

Dead in the West, 1993, 2 issues (adapted by Neal Barrett Jr.; art by Jack Jackson; covers by Tim Truman)

By Bizarre Hands, 1994, 3 issues (adaptations by Neal Barrett Jr. and Jerry Prosser; art by Phil Hester and Dean Rohrer)

Atomic Chili: The Illustrated Joe Lansdale, 1996

"Bob the Dinosaur Goes to Disneyland" (adapted by Rick Klaw; art by Doug Potter) (First publication at RevolutionSF, 2001; first book publication in *Geek Confidential: Echoes From the 21st Century*, 2003, by Rick Klaw)

Lansdale & Truman's Dead Folks, 2003, 3 issues (from the story "On the Far Side of the Cadillac Desert with Dead Folks")

The Drive-In, 2003, 4 issues (adapted by Chris Golden; art by Andres Guinaldo)

By Bizarre Hands, 2004, 6 issues (adaptations by Neal Barrett Jr., Keith Lansdale, and Rick Klaw; art by Dheeraj Verma, Armando Rossi, and Andres Guinaldo)

The Drive-In 2, 2006, 4 issues (adapted by Neal Barrett Jr.; art by Andres Guinaldo)

"Incident on and off a Mountain Road" in *Masters of Horror* #1–2, 2006 (adapted by Chris Ryall)

Anthologies edited

The Best of the West, 1989

New Frontier, 1989

Razored Saddles, 1989 (with Pat Lobrutto)

Dark at Heart, 1991 (with Karen Lansdale)

Weird Business: A Horror Comics Anthology, 1995 (with
     Richard Klaw)

The West That Was, 1994 (with Thomas Knowles)

Wild West Show, 1994 (with Thomas Knowles)

The Horror Hall of Fame: The Stoker Winners, 2004

Retro-Pulp Tales, 2006

Lords of the Razor, 2006

Cross Plains Universe: Texans Celebrate Robert E. Howard,
     2006 (with Scott A. Cupp)

Son of Retro Pulp Tales, 2009 (with Keith Lansdale)

Crucified Dreams, 2010

The Urban Fantasy Anthology, 2011 (with Peter S. Beagle)

ABOUT THE AUTHOR

JOE R. LANSDALE IS the author of over forty novels and three hundred short pieces—fiction, nonfiction, essays, and reviews. He has written numerous screenplays and teleplays. Among those are scripts for *Batman: The Animated Series*, *Superman: The Animated Series*, animated short films for DC Showcase, and the animated film *Son of Batman*. His work has been filmed by others, including the films *Bubba Ho-Tep*, *Cold in July*, *Christmas with the Dead*, "Incident on and off a Mountain Road" for Showtime's *Masters of Horror*, and the Sundance television series *Hap and Leonard*, based on his popular crime novels. Other works of his are in preproduction, including *The Pit*, *The Thicket*, with Peter Dinklage, and *The Bottoms*, coproduced and directed by fellow Texan Bill Paxton. Other novels and stories are under option.

He is the recipient of numerous awards, among them the Edgar for Best Crime Novel, the Herodotus for Best Historical Crime Novel, the Inkpot Award for Lifetime Achievement in Science Fiction and Fantasy, the Grinzane Cavour Prize for literature, the British Fantasy Award, the Golden Lion Award for contributions to the works of Edgar Rice Burroughs, ten Bram Stokers, one of which is a Lifetime Achievement Award, the Grandmaster of Horror Award, and the Mid-South Award. He is a member of the Texas Institute of Letters, the Texas Literary Hall of Fame, and is writer-in-residence at Stephen F. Austin State University. He is the founder/grandmaster of Shen Chuan, Martial Science, and Shen Chuan Family System and has been recognized by the International Martial Arts Hall of Fame. He teaches private lessons at his dojo in Nacogdoches, Texas, and conducts occasional martial arts seminars and camps.

His children are Keith Lansdale, also an author and screen and comic writer, and Kasey Lansdale, professional musician, writer, and actress. Lansdale lives in Nacogdoches with his wife Karen, writer, editor, and manager. He has a pit bull named Nicky, who does not write or do anything artistic. So far.

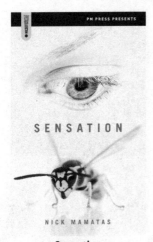

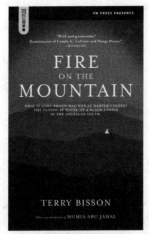

Also available from PM Press

Report from Planet Midnight
NALO HOPKINSON
ISBN: 978-1-60486-497-7
$12.00

The Science of Herself
KAREN JOY FOWLER
ISBN: 978-1-60486-825-8
$12.00

Raising Hell
NORMAN SPINRAD
ISBN: 978-1-60486-810-4
$12.00

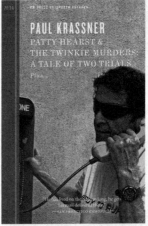

**Patty Hearst & The Twinkie Murders:
A Tale of Two Trials**
PAUL KRASSNER
ISBN: 978-1-629630-38-0
$12.00

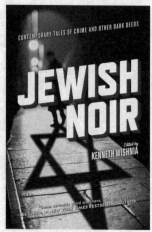

Jewish Noir
EDITED BY KENNETH WISHNIA
ISBN: 978-1-62963-111-0
$17.95

Late in the Day: Poems 2010–2014
URSULA K. LE GUIN
ISBN: 978-1-62963-122-6
$18.95

Cazzarola!: Anarchy,
Romani, Love, Italy
NORMAN NAWROCKI
ISBN: 978-1-60486-315-4
$18.00

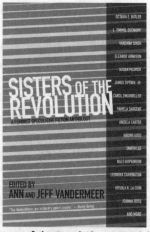

Sisters of the Revolution: A Feminist
Speculative Fiction Anthology
EDITED BY ANN AND JEFF VANDERMEER
ISBN: 978-1-62963-035-9
$15.95

FRIENDS OF

PM

These are indisputably momentous times—the financial system is melting down globally and the Empire is stumbling. Now more than ever there is a vital need for radical ideas.

In the eight years since its founding—and on a mere shoestring—PM Press has risen to the formidable challenge of publishing and distributing knowledge and entertainment for the struggles ahead. With hundreds of releases to date, we have published an impressive and stimulating array of literature, art, music, politics, and culture. Using every available medium, we've succeeded in connecting those hungry for ideas and information to those putting them into practice.

Friends of PM allows you to directly help impact, amplify, and revitalize the discourse and actions of radical writers, filmmakers, and artists. It provides us with a stable foundation from which we can build upon our early successes and provides a much-needed subsidy for the materials that can't necessarily pay their own way. You can help make that happen—and receive every new title automatically delivered to your door once a month—by joining as a Friend of PM Press. And, we'll throw in a free T-shirt when you sign up.

Here are your options:

- $30 a month: Get all books and pamphlets plus 50% discount on all webstore purchases
- $40 a month: Get all PM Press releases (including CDs and DVDs) plus 50% discount on all webstore purchases
- $100 a month: Superstar—Everything plus PM merchandise, free downloads, and 50% discount on all webstore purchases

For those who can't afford $30 or more a month, we're introducing Sustainer Rates at $15, $10, and $5. Sustainers get a free PM Press T-shirt and a 50% discount on all purchases from our website.

Your Visa or Mastercard will be billed once a month, until you tell us to stop. Or until our efforts succeed in bringing the revolution around. Or the financial meltdown of Capital makes plastic redundant. Whichever comes first.

PM Press was founded at the end of 2007 by a small collection of folks with decades of publishing, media, and organizing experience. PM Press co-conspirators have published and distributed hundreds of books, pamphlets, CDs, and DVDs. Members of PM have founded enduring book fairs, spearheaded victorious tenant organizing campaigns, and worked closely with bookstores, academic conferences, and even rock bands to deliver political and challenging ideas to all walks of life. We're old enough to know what we're doing and young enough to know what's at stake.

We seek to create radical and stimulating fiction and non-fiction books, pamphlets, t-shirts, visual and audio materials to entertain, educate, and inspire you. We aim to distribute these through every available channel with every available technology—whether that means you are seeing anarchist classics at our bookfair stalls; reading our latest vegan cookbook at the café; downloading geeky fiction e-books; or digging new music and timely videos from our website.

PM Press is always on the lookout for talented and skilled volunteers, artists, activists, and writers to work with. If you have a great idea for a project or can contribute in some way, please get in touch.

PM Press
PO Box 23912
Oakland CA 94623
510-658-3906
www.pmpress.org